Love at First Cowboy

 Horseshoe Home Ranch

LIZ ISAACSON

ISBN-13: 978-1-63876-245-4

*Judge not, and ye shall not be judged: condemn not, and ye
shall not be condemned: forgive, and ye shall be forgiven."*

— LUKE 6:37

CHAPTER 1

$\mathcal{E}$lliott Hawthorne opened the cabin door to a blast of air conditioning—thankfully—and the sight of Archer taping the top of a box. Unthankfully.

"Hey." He sighed and straightened his back with a groan. "You're still helping me move tonight, right?"

Elliott didn't want to, but as he closed the door behind him so he wouldn't air condition the ranch with all its September heat, he said, "Yeah."

"Don't sound so happy about it."

"I'm not happy about it." Elliott tried to smile to soften the words. "And I'm totally jealous you're going up to Landon's cabin on Bear Mountain."

Archer smiled, reminding Elliott why they'd gotten along so well as roommates. "So it's nice?"

Elliott also reminded himself that they would still be friends. Co-workers too. So Archer was getting married. Big deal. It was what adults did.

Well, everyone except for Elliott at least.

"It's really nice," Elliott said. "It's small, but intimate, and quiet, and it's a great place to relax and unwind." He wished he could go right now. Take his bay horse Precious with him and go. Skip Archer moving out. Skip Archer and Emery's wedding. Skip the whole Labor Day picnic—which he would attend alone. Again.

But the ranch was buzzing with all of the above. The cowboys didn't get off the ranch much in the late summer and early fall because of the harvest, but Ty, the foreman, had announced last week that minimal chores would be done on Labor Day and no one was allowed to come back until evening.

Elliott was planning to attend the picnic with the cowboys, and then he'd probably go visit his parents. He didn't get down to see them much because of his workload, but they were starting to get older and he knew he needed to make more of an effort to help them.

With two of his brothers already living in other cities, and one preparing to sell his carpet cleaning company and relocate, Elliott would be the only son left in Gold Valley soon enough.

"Need some help?" he asked as he unwrapped a granola bar. He didn't like to eat a lot for lunch, especially when it was really hot outside.

"I think I'm good," Archer said. "I moved up here with just two truckloads, so it shouldn't take long."

"You're buying me dinner after, right?" Elliott grinned at him.

Archer rolled his eyes. "Steak, if I remember your conditions."

"Hey, I have to drive you to the church tomorrow too," he said, scowling. "I deserve steak."

Archer's expression turned sympathetic, and Elliott hated it. He appreciated it too, but he really didn't need Archer's pity.

"So Andra didn't work out." He wasn't really asking.

"She…wasn't my type." Elliott was starting to think he didn't have a type. That no matter how many women he went out with, none of them would ever be a fit for him.

He'd had some luck with women in his early twenties, but the last five years had been a painful stretch of being single punctuated with first date after disastrous first date.

"Emery can check around better this time," Archer said, but Elliott shook his head and took off his black cowboy hat.

"I'm not interested in getting set up again," he said. "No more blind dates, no more friend-of-a-friend, none of it." Elliott's brown hair flopped around and he picked up his phone to text his barber. Maybe he could squeeze in a haircut between moving and the steak.

With the appointment set and his granola bar gone, Elliott left Archer to finish the packing and went back out to the ranch.

That evening, it took Elliott and Archer thirty minutes to load the boxes, clothes, and Archer's bed into two pickup trucks. "See you down there," Archer said, climbing behind the wheel of his smaller truck.

Elliott lifted his hand and got into his ranch truck to follow Archer to Emery's townhome. Another thirty minutes passed during the drive. Another thirty to get everything unloaded. Another thirty for the haircut.

Elliott was starting to wonder if he could just continue in this pattern. Thirty minute increments where he didn't have to worry about being single, where no one asked him who he was dating, where he didn't have to concern himself with meeting someone.

It sounded like a good plan, and he immediately adopted it.

Another thirty minutes later, he had his prime rib in front of him, a beautiful mid-rare cook on the meat and a pile of garlic mashed potatoes that made his mouth water. He ate the green beans and baby carrots because his mother had trained him to eat his vegetables and he'd trained himself to get that part over with first.

Archer asked questions about the cabin, and they talked about the ranch, and Elliott, drowsy on steak and potatoes, decided that it wasn't so bad that he'd be getting a new roommate in a couple of weeks. That he'd have to live alone until then.

Thank you for allowing me to be happy for him, Elliott thought as Archer set his credit card on the bill.

His phone rang, and Elliott checked the screen. "It's my brother," he said to Archer. "I'll meet you outside." He stood and swiped open the call. "Hey, Joel."

"Elliott."

With that one word, Elliott's insides iced. The food he'd eaten—which was a lot—solidified into cement.

"What's wrong?"

"Mom just called. Dad's fallen down and they're on their way to the hospital."

"Fell down? Where? How long ago?" He frantically patted his pockets to find his keys. Archer had planned to leave his truck at Emery's and ride back up the canyon with Elliott, but new arrangements would have to be made.

"About half an hour ago, and he was going to do some work in the backyard."

Guilt pulled through Elliott with the force of gravity. His father shouldn't be doing yard work; Elliott should've been going down and helping his parents out, the way Ty had been for the past few years.

"I'm on my way," he told Joel, turning back to talk to Archer.

One thirty-minute increment later, Elliott finally found his brother in the emergency waiting room. They embraced, and Elliott didn't like the worry in his brother's brown eyes. "Broken hip," Joel said. "He's going into surgery within the hour."

Two increments, Elliott thought. He could wait that long. Wait and worry, which was exactly what he did. His mother —his petite, sandy-haired mother—came through the doors only fifty-two minutes later. She'd been crying, and Elliott swamped her in a tight hug, his own emotions threatening to overflow.

"He's okay," she said as they all sat down in the waiting

area. "There's no reason for you boys to wait here. It's getting late. Go on home and get some rest."

Neither Joel nor Elliott moved. They exchanged a glance, and Joel leaned forward. "Ma, why don't you let Elliott take you home? He'll stay with you and I'll wait here to talk to the doctors when they come out of surgery."

Mom started shaking her head before Joel could even finish speaking, and Elliott knew she'd never leave Dad here.

Joel tried again anyway. "Mom, he'll be in there for a few hours. Elliott will bring you back when they finish."

Elliott put his hand on his mother's. "Ma, come on." To his surprise, she rose to her feet and went with him. Elliott tossed a look over his shoulder to his older brother, who nodded with a sad smile.

———

A week later, Elliott woke in the cabin by himself. He made a pot of coffee for himself, something Archer had been doing for nine months. He wasn't a morning person, so he'd let Archer set the alarms, make the coffee, and get them out the door. But he had to do all that himself now.

He'd been down to the valley every evening since his father's fall. His dad had been released from the hospital yesterday, and Joel had called late last night to ask Elliott to come down again tonight to meet the nursing staff that would be assisting their father for the next several months.

"I can't be there after the end of the month," Joel said. "I need you to handle it."

Elliott didn't want to handle it. He was the youngest of the four boys, and the only one not married. He worked twelve hours a day, and adding the care of his parents to his plate felt like it was going to choke him.

But he made it through the twelve hours and down the canyon to his parents' house. Joel's car was already there, as were two other vehicles, leaving Elliott to park on the street.

Get through this one increment, he coached himself before he entered the house, the familiar smell of marinara meeting his nose. His mother had likely been cooking all day, adding her tears into the homemade sauce while she waited for evening and her sons to come.

"Elliott," his mom said, coming down the hall from the great room where he assumed everyone would be. She drew him into a tight hug. "We're just fine," she whispered.

He drew back, confused. "Who says you aren't?"

"Elliott's here," Joel said before she could answer, and he joined them, drawing Mom back into the great room. Elliott followed, unsure of what he'd find once he rounded the corner.

The kitchen stretched to his right, with a dining set in front of a pair of French doors that led into the backyard. Four steps went down—the site of his father's fall.

A big living room filled the rest of space, with a large sectional that held Joel's wife and two kids on the longest side and two women on the shorter one.

Elliott's gaze landed on a woman with silver-purple hair that only reached her chin. It was very straight, not a hair out of place. She turned toward him, and everything around him fell away.

Only her brown eyes existed. Her heart-shaped face. Her timid yet strong smile.

Elliott needed to know her name, right now. Find out how she got her hair to fall like that. Her skin reminded him of the shimmery-white way the horizon shone when the sun was at its pinnacle, and he wanted to touch her, stat.

Everything rushed forward again, and Elliott managed to smile when Joel introduced the dark-haired woman next to the exotic beauty who'd rendered him breathless with a single look.

"And this is Holland Marsh," Joel said. "She's a physical therapist from the home health center."

Holland Marsh. Even her name was sexy, and Elliott reached out to shake her hand.

"Nice to meet you," she said, painting his world in glorious colors just with her voice.

His heart pounded, nearly romping around in his chest like a bull gone rogue. He felt ridiculous—or like he'd been transported back in time fifteen years, when he was ruled by first impressions and strong hormones.

"Hey, Dad," he managed to say, bending down to give his father a quick, soft hug. "I see Ma's made her spaghetti and meatballs."

His father smiled though Elliott knew he was in a lot of pain, and said, "You know how she is."

Elliott did, and he cut a quick glance at the violet-haired Holland, who wore a patient and kind smile for his dad. "She likes to cook for a crowd."

"Elliott," Joel said. "Since Demmie and I are moving to Sacramento, you'll need to sign the power of attorney papers."

Elliott tore his gaze from Holland, wrenched his mind away from his fully formed fantasies. "I'm sorry," he said. "Power of attorney?" He glanced at his mother, who stood with her arms cinched across her chest, everything making sense now.

Joel also watched their mom for a moment before turning back to Elliott with a long, impatient sigh. "They need help."

"With the yard," Elliott said. "The snow. The weeds." He normally didn't argue with anyone, but something told him this was wrong. "Joel, they're mentally sound. Dad just broke his hip. He didn't hit his head."

"I'm fine," Dad said, his voice barely audible.

"We're fine," Mom added, giving Elliott all the fuel he needed to see this through to the end.

"You go on to Sacramento," Elliott said. "I'll take care of Mom and Dad."

Joel looked like he wanted to argue. Instead, he stepped past Elliott and perched on the arm of the couch by his wife, Demmie. "Holland?" he asked.

"Your father needs a lot of care," the beautiful woman said, making Elliott's pulse zing through him like someone had hooked him up to a huge battery.

"I'm here," Mom said. "Elliott will come down from the ranch in the evenings. And you ladies will be here."

"Just one nurse, ma'am." Holland looked apologetic as she said it, her eyes filled with tenderness. "Your insurance only covers *one* home health nurse."

"We'll be fine," Mom said again, this time with a note of pleading in her tone.

Elliott met Holland's eyes, but she didn't give him an indication of what he should do. He did want the best medical care for his father.

"How about we just see how they do?" Elliott asked, swinging his gaze from his mother, to Holland, and to Joel. "Give them a couple of months and see how things go."

He looked hopefully back to Holland, as if she alone had the power to make this decision. Or maybe he just wanted to absorb the beauty of her face again.

She clasped her hands and gave him a small smile before ducking her head toward the other woman. "We'll leave you. See you tomorrow, Mister Hawthorne," she said to his father. She moved toward the corner, and Elliott's heart screamed at him to *go with her! Follow her! Get her phone number!*

"I'll be right back," he said to the room and went with them. "Excuse me?" he asked, causing both women to turn back.

"How often will you come?" he asked.

"The nurse will come a few times a week," Holland explained. "The physical therapist comes as often as the insurance will let me. In the beginning, that will be every day."

"What time?" He hoped he wasn't being too obvious, but he also really needed to know.

"Your brother has everything to explain the physical therapy," Holland said, not unkindly. In fact, she seemed good, and kind, and caring. She seemed strong, and capable, and sure of herself. Elliott wondered if that was his type. He sure hoped so.

"One more question," he said as she opened the door. "*You'll* be coming to do the physical therapy?"

A smile formed fully on her face, and Elliott almost got knocked backward from the brilliance of it. "No one has been assigned yet," she said. "We meet in the morning."

Elliott's heart plummeted, but he kept his face placid. "Okay, thanks," he said, his mind racing. At least he had one night to beg God to assign Holland to his father's care.

CHAPTER 2

Holland Marsh thought about the handsome cowboy that had blown into the Hawthorne house as she drove home. She didn't know anything about him, but something in his happy-hazel eyes had ignited something in her soul that had died when she'd left Idaho Falls.

Before that, actually. She'd simply decided to do something about the dead feelings inside, and that had prompted the move from everything she'd known in Idaho to Gold Valley, Montana, where her aunt and uncle had lived for thirty years.

Uncle Wallace had tried to get her a job at the equine rehabilitation center where he was the director, but she didn't have the right letters behind her name. Didn't matter. She'd gotten a job at a home health center easily enough. Seemed Montana had a shortage of physical therapists just like most other places.

She pulled into her cousin's driveway, her mind lingering on the black cowboy hat Elliott Hawthorne had been wearing. She tucked the image of him into the back of her mind to consider later, when she was alone again.

Cecil looked up from the stove where he had something delicious cooking. "Ah, there you are," he said with a smile. Recently divorced, he'd been enthusiastic about having her stay with him while she got her bearings in Gold Valley.

She'd been here for six months and certainly had her bearings, but she hadn't moved out. She and Cecil got along great. He cooked; she did dishes. They both liked Chinese food on Friday nights, and sitting near the back in church on Sundays. And Holland could admit she liked having a friend to come home to at night.

Her labradoodle Lucy came barreling toward the back door, and Holland cooed at her as the dog's whole body wagged back and forth in excitement.

She scrubbed the curly hair on top of Lucy's head. "How are you, you big sheep?" With a big barrel body, her white coloring, and that curly poodle hair, Lucy really did resemble a sheep more than a dog.

Lucy put her paws on Holland's chest, but Holland pushed her down. "Stop it, you moose." She grinned at the dog and pulled the back door closed.

She exhaled heavily as she sat at the bar. "What's that?" she asked, eying the mixture in the pan. It looked like—

"Mushrooms and onions and chicken," he said. "For the calzones."

"Calzones? People actually make those?"

Cecil chuckled and balanced the wooden spoon on the pan's edge to turn his attention to the dough on the counter. He patted it, spooned on the filling, and sealed the pockets expertly. As he slid the tray of egg-washed calzones into a hot oven, Holland reminded herself that he worked in a supermarket all day.

So he was the grocery manager, doing everything from schedules to payroll to ordering, not a chef or anything. But he certainly knew food and how to put it together, for which Holland was grateful. She hadn't had the energy to put more together than bread and peanut butter since her move.

Before that, really. One day she'd admit that everything in her life had changed when she'd started dating Jordan Mickelson.

But that wasn't today, and she leaned into her palms as Cecil started stacking dishes in the sink for her to wash later. "So I met someone today."

He froze, only his eyes moving up to meet hers. "In the home health center? What did we establish about dating patients?"

Holland gave her cousin a smile. "He's not a patient." Because they had established a strict no-dating-patients rule for Holland. "He's a cowboy."

Cecil quirked one eyebrow at her. "How did you meet a cowboy?"

"His father broke his hip. He came down for the family consult." The scent of baking bread filled the house, and Holland took a deep breath, thinking of her mother's cooking.

"So you spoke to him for five seconds," Cecil said, shaking his head. "I know this game."

"He was handsome."

"I thought you were here to work. Get your career started. In fact, I distinctly remember you saying the words 'No dating for me. No sir. Not necessary.'" He settled against the counter opposite her and smirked.

"It's *not* necessary," Holland said, an air of forced nonchalance in her tone. Dating in general wasn't necessary, but dating Elliott Hawthorne…. Well, she'd do everything she could to get assigned to his father, as Elliott would be coming down from the ranch where he worked every evening and she really wanted to know what color of hair hid beneath that delicious cowboy hat.

––––––––

With a chicken and mushroom calzone in her lunchbox, Holland headed into work the next morning earlier than usual. Only ten minutes, but enough to get to the center, stash her lunch, and be in the conference room before anyone else. She was usually one of the last, bustling in with her coffee and an apologetic smile to the director.

But not today. Oh, no. She wanted to be seen first when Kevin walked through the door, maybe even ask about Sean Hawthorne.

With four new cases being assigned today and only two

physical therapists, Holland had a good chance of landing the Hawthorne case.

"Morning, Holland," Kevin said as he entered the room. He carried several folders, and Holland put on her brightest smile and didn't look at what he had in his arms.

"Morning."

"How did things go with the family consult last night?" He sat at the head of the table and pulled a pen out of his breast pocket.

"Great," she said, maybe a little too brightly. "The younger son didn't want to sign the power of attorney."

"That's fine." Kevin didn't even glance up from the paperwork.

"I liked the father," Holland said, though Char had done most of the work with him last night. She was a CNA and had taken the vitals and marked the chart.

"Great." Kevin fanned the folders and tapped one. "Do you want him?"

Holland lifted one shoulder though Kevin hadn't even looked up. "Sure, I'll take him."

He pushed the folder toward her and marked something on his clipboard. "Sounds good. He needs to be seen today."

Holland didn't reach for the folder, though she wanted to grab it and press it to her chest. "I'll schedule a time to get over there."

Two nurses entered the room and Holland fell silent. She'd gotten what she'd wanted, and a giggle threatened to escape her lips. She kept it contained during the meeting, but as soon as she got to her closet of an office, she couldn't help letting it out.

———

"Yes, definitely let your son know what time I'm coming," Holland said later that morning, after calling Sean Hawthorne to set up his physical therapy appointment. "Since I've only been approved to come three times a week, you'll need to do the therapy on your own, and I'd like to train your wife and son so they can help you."

"All right," Sean said. "He works a lot. If he needs to be here, evenings are best."

"I can accommodate your schedule, Mister Hawthorne." Holland wore a smile on her face that translated into her voice.

"Maybe you should call him," Sean said. "I don't know when he'll be done tonight."

Holland's heart started beating to a quick rhythm. "What time is good for you?" she asked. After all, she was getting paid to rehabilitate Sean Hawthorne, not arrange a time to meet his son.

"Anytime that works for Elliott works for us," he said. "Here's his number." He recited the number, and Holland hastened to scratch it on a nearby scrap of paper.

"I'll give him a call," she promised before hanging up.

But she didn't call right away. She wanted to, but she didn't want her excitement to show in her voice. She needed to be professional, aloof, the way she'd been last night.

Business during business hours, she reminded herself.

Still, she waited until she'd consumed her calzone before even attempting to call Elliott. She hadn't called a cute cowboy before, and though she had sworn off dating when she'd left Idaho, her stomach was still a jittery mess.

Properly fed, with carbs in her system, she punched in the necessary numbers. His phone rang and rang, finally going to voicemail. She'd only heard him speak a few words, but when he said, "This is Elliott Hawthorne. I'm probably out of range right now, so leave a message, and I'll call you back," her pulse picked up.

He had a deep, sexy voice that made the hair on the back of her neck stand up. He'd been tall, trim, and tough in the way he'd denied his older brother over the power of attorney.

She cleared her throat just as the beep sounded on his voicemail. "Hello, Elliott," she said in her calmest voice possible. "This is Holland Marsh…."

CHAPTER 3

"Hello, Elliott," Holland's voice on his phone said. "This is Holland Marsh. I'm trying to set up my first appointment with your father, and I believe it's important you be there. I'll only be able to come three times a week for him, and I want to train you and your mother in the physical therapy he needs. Would this evening work for you? If so, please call and let me know what time. Thanks."

She started listing the digits of her phone number, and Elliott just stood there. Just stood there in his near-empty cowboy cabin, pure shock flowing through him.

The message ended, and a smile lifted his lips.

Would this evening work for you?

Heck, yeah, this evening worked for him. He pressed one to replay the message, not only to get her number but to hear the sweet sound of her voice again.

He wasn't sure who he was. He didn't get all worked up

over a woman the moment he met her. He never had. But he certainly was worked up over Holland Marsh, and he wasn't even sure why.

"Hey, Miss Marsh," he said when she answered. "It's Elliott Hawthorne."

She cleared her throat. "Oh, hello, Elliott."

He liked the way she said his name, clean and crisp, without an accent. "What time this evening?" He thought through the rest of the chores he needed to finish. It was close to three o'clock, and he probably had three more hours to go.

"Anytime that works for you."

"How about seven?" he asked. That would give him thirty minutes to shower. Thirty minutes to drive down the canyon. Maybe he should've gone for seven-thirty so he could have thirty minutes to eat.

"Seven is fine," she said, her voice a bit cool.

"You know what? Let's do seven-thirty. I need to grab something to eat on the way down."

"Oh, I—" She cut off, but Elliott really wanted to know what she would've said.

She remained silent, so he said, "See you tonight."

She agreed, and he ended the call, sinking onto his couch with the silent device in his hand. No, he hadn't asked her out on a date, but his heart raced like he had. His muscles had tightened and then collapsed like he had.

He had no idea why this woman affected him so strongly —but he had seven thirty-minute increments to figure it out and then hide it so his mother wouldn't see him acting like a fool tonight. Then he'd have double the questions to answer than he normally did.

Seven-thirty came quickly. With such an exciting thing happening that night, the time increments seemed to pass in a single breath.

He arrived at his parents' house and parked his truck next to a black sedan he'd seen last night. Elliott unwrapped a peppermint, stuck it in his mouth to eradicate any scent of his western barbeque burger dinner, and reminded himself to *walk* up to the front door.

With his nerves firing, he almost knocked on the door. At the last moment, he pulled his fist back and twisted the knob the way he'd been doing since he moved out. Voices from the back of the house echoed toward him, and he slicked his palms down the front of his jeans before rounding the corner to find his dad standing next to his mom in the kitchen.

They faced Holland, who stood with her back to Elliott. Her laugh rang through the space in the next moment, and her super-straight hair fell back as her head tipped, revealing that part of her head had been shaved along the sides.

Elliott found everything about her shocking, alluring, and unique. His fingers itched to touch her scalp, preferably while he kissed her.

"Hey," he said, his voice on the squeaky end of things. He noticed his father leaning into the counter instead of really supporting himself, and concern replaced his fantasies about Holland. Simply being in the same room as her satisfied him—for now.

She turned toward him, her hand flying to her hair to smooth it down, though it was lying perfectly flat already.

"Elliott." His mother moved around the kitchen island to embrace him. He grinned as he hugged her. "You should've come for dinner."

"I had to work," he said, the same excuse he'd used dozens of times. "I grabbed a hamburger." He caught Holland watching him, and his throat turned dry. He wished he'd grabbed his soda before coming in.

"So let's get started." Holland ducked her head, that silver hair falling over the side of her face. Elliott wanted to brush it back, look into those dreamy brown eyes, and—he broke off his thoughts as she drew his father around the counter too.

He moved in herky jerky motions, and Elliott's heart pinched. He wanted to help his father. *Remember why you're here*, he reprimanded himself.

"So you, Sean," Holland said. "Will need to do these exercises several times a day. And Doctor Rutledge wants you in outpatient therapy on the days I don't come." She gave his father a warm smile, and heat shot through Elliott.

She demonstrated the toe touches, with the help of his dad's walker. "Or another stable surface," she said. "And you'll need to walk. Flat surfaces are best, so you'll just have to navigate the steps in the garage or the front porch." She looked at Elliott and then his mom. "He should never go down stairs by himself. Position yourself in front of him, because that's the direction he'll fall if he becomes unsteady."

She locked eyes with Elliott again, and a charge bounced between them. The silence stretched long enough for his mother to look from him to Holland and back. A small part of Elliott died, and he ground the attraction flowing between them from his throat.

"So let's go," Holland said, a beautiful blush creeping into her cheeks and making her hair seem even whiter. "Garage or front door, Sean?"

"Garage." His dad seemed to be perspiring already, and he leaned heavily on his walker as he followed Holland with painful steps toward the door leading into the garage. She waited until he'd crowded her on the landing, and then she eased down three steps.

"All right," she said. "Gently now." She took the walker and put it solidly on the next step down. "Very little weight on the injured side. Step with it first. Rest all your weight on the walker." She steadied the walker too, and down they went, step by step, until his father reached the solid garage floor.

"Excellent, Sean." She beamed at him like he'd just won a marathon. "Now, I believe your wife mentioned a duck pond."

"To the right," his father panted as he headed toward the end of the driveway.

Holland let him go on ahead, and Elliott paused next to her, barely standing outside of the garage. "Always give him a choice," she said quietly to him and his mother. "He'll feel powerless enough as it is. Ask him if he wants to go out the front door or the garage. If he wants to walk to the duck pond or the park over on Keller Avenue." She folded her arms and smiled in his father's direction.

"Three short walks each day. Fifteen or twenty minutes." She took a step and everyone moved with her. "And let him get up and get things for himself." She reached over and touched his mom's arm. "I know that's hard for you, but it will help him heal faster."

"I'll try."

"Ma," Elliott said, wanting to be helpful and not really knowing how.

"I'll try, Elliott." She quickened her step and reached his father after only a few seconds. Elliott expected Holland to do the same, give more instructions, but she didn't. She matched her pace to his, which was as slow as his injured father's. He had no desire to catch up to his parents, and as the sun continued to set, a sense of contentment poured over Elliott.

"So you didn't grow up here," he said, keeping his gaze forward.

"No," she said. "But my aunt and uncle have lived here for thirty years, and when I was looking to…relocate, this seemed like a good fit." She lifted her shoulders in a long, deep breath in and then exhaled. "I've always loved Gold Valley." She trained her eyes on his, and he couldn't help smiling.

"I have too."

"You did grow up here."

"Right there in that house." He chuckled and stuffed his hands in his pockets so he wouldn't reach for her. "I live and work up at Horseshoe Home Ranch now."

"Horseshoe Home."

"There are four ranches up the canyon. We're the first one." Elliott wasn't sure why he was telling her that. She wouldn't make the drive up to the ranch to see him. Why would she?

"I live right there." She nodded to the last house on the opposite side of the street, the one with green shutters and a fresh coat of gray paint.

"That's Cecil Richards's place," he said, not following.

"He's my cousin," Holland said, peering at the house.

"And you live with him."

"Yeah." She sighed and pulled her gaze from the house. "He got divorced about a year ago, and I got into town six months ago. It's nice not to have to go home alone." Vulnerability raced through her expression, and she covered it with a razor-thin smile.

"I get it," Elliott said. "My cabin mate just got married and moved out last weekend." The pressure in his chest increased. "I don't have a new one yet."

"Cabin mate?"

"Yeah. We cowboys have to share up at the ranch."

"You love working at the ranch."

He caught her eye, and they both paused. "Sure do. Listen, do you wanna, I mean, maybe we could grab something to eat together sometime." Elliott's thoughts rebounded around inside his skull. Had he just asked her out? Just like that?

"I'd like that." She tucked her hair behind her ear and started strolling again. She'd accepted, just like that. So he hadn't imagined the connection between them.

"Why did you want to relocate?" he asked.

"Needed a fresh start," she said. "After a bad break-up." She nudged him with her shoulder. "Nothing serious."

"You left your hometown over a guy and it wasn't serious?" Elliott didn't believe that. Someone like Holland didn't do not-serious, he could just tell. He enjoyed the way they spoke, like they weren't asking questions but stating obvious facts about the other.

"It was serious," she said. "Look, maybe we can talk about it at dinner tomorrow night." She smiled and giggled, but the sound held a lot of anxiety. "Give me some time to figure out how much to tell you."

"I want to know all of it." He took a big step in front of her and stopped, forcing her to pause too. "Holland, I—" He couldn't get himself to articulate how he felt. He didn't know how he felt. He'd never felt like this before, never had this love-at-first-sight experience ricocheting inside his chest.

He cast a quick glance over his shoulder to see where his parents were. Not even to the corner yet. Not concerned about where Holland and Elliott were.

Nothing else seemed to be stirring in the neighborhood. Elliott wasn't sure what to say, but he knew what he wanted to do.

He leaned closer, bent his head toward hers, and said, "Tomorrow night," before brushing his lips against hers for the briefest of kisses. Everything inside him wanted to claim her mouth as his, but he forced himself backward, away from her, utterly stunned at what he'd done.

Her hand moved as if in slow motion to lightly touch her lips. She seemed as frozen as he felt, and Elliott cursed himself for his forward, assuming behavior.

He ducked his head, using his cowboy hat to conceal his face, and turned to catch his parents. His lips tingled and ached for more contact with hers, but all he could give them was a smile. A hopeful smile that tomorrow he could provide them with what they wanted: a proper kiss with Holland Marsh.

Somehow, Holland made it through the next hour with the Hawthorne's, the ghost of Elliott's lips still skating across hers. He'd barely touched her, and yet it was the most exciting kiss she'd ever experienced.

Why is that? she asked herself as she watched him drive away in his truck with a double-H logo on the driver's side door. She wasn't sure, but she hoped she'd find out at dinner the next evening.

She walked to her car, a slight bounce in her step and an inexplicable excitement way down deep in her core. She could barely contain herself when she burst into Cecil's house. He sat on the couch in the living room, a binder open in front of him. His scheduling binder.

"Elliott Hawthorne kissed me," she said, pressing her back into the closed front door.

Cecil abandoned his binder and leapt to his feet. "He did *what?*" he asked, like kissing was a scandalous thing to do.

Well, maybe it was when she barely knew the guy. Had only met him twenty-four hours ago. Still, she *felt* something between them, something *for* him she'd never felt with anyone before.

"I mean, it was barely a kiss. Really more of a brush of his lips. A whisper, almost." Still, her fingers drifted to her mouth again, like they could feel his kiss there. "We're going to dinner tomorrow night."

She practically skipped around the couch and collapsed onto it, dislodging his binder a little.

"I can't believe you."

"What?"

"A kiss *before* the first date." He grinned and shook his head. "For Gold Valley, this is the most scandalous thing that's happened in years."

Holland laughed. "It was barely a kiss."

"But he likes you."

"Apparently."

"So at least the attraction goes both ways." Cecil took his spot on the couch again. "All I've got is this *thrilling* binder." He bent over it again, his mouth curving up a little.

Holland let him get back to work, scheduling produce workers for the next two weeks. She disappeared inside her own mind, but she wasn't alone. Oh, no. Elliott was there, and he was strong, safe, and sexy.

She'd always wondered if love at first sight existed, and she had the barest of inklings now that it did.

Still, it would be smart to get to know him first.

He's not Jordan, she told herself. He cared about his

parents, for one. He was employed, for two. And he hadn't dated her sister, for three.

Yeah, Elliott had a lot going for him that Holland liked.

———

The next day, she worked with four clients, none of them Sean Hawthorne. Holland enjoyed her job; she always had. Seeing the strides people made as they came back from devastating accidents and injuries brought her so much joy. She'd also learned gratitude from her patients. Gratitude for her own health. Gratitude for her good fortune.

Even when Jordan had ripped her heart out and sliced it open, Holland had known she would recover. She just didn't want it happen in Idaho Falls.

She returned home for a quick shower, realizing as she towel-dried her hair that she had no idea where or when she was meeting Elliott. He didn't have her personal phone number, and she'd written down his at work. The thought of going back to her office at the home health center— clear across town—didn't appeal to her. Eating something spicy for dinner certainly did. But not alone. Oh, no. She really wanted to sit across from Elliott and bask in the warmth of his smile, maybe reach across the table and hold his hand as he told her about his job, his family, his life.

She'd shown him where she lived, but they hadn't made plans for him to pick her up. A quick glance at the clock showed her that it was only six o'clock. He'd requested seven-thirty the previous night, and she told herself to be patient.

Her phone rang, and she automatically flinched toward it. But it wasn't Elliott.

Mom sat on the screen, and Holland couldn't let the call go unanswered. "Hey, Mom," she said.

"Holland." Her mom sounded good, and relief rushed through Holland. She had good days and bad days since Holland's father had passed away almost two years ago. Time was said to heal all wounds, but it worked slower on some than others.

"How's your job going?" her mom asked.

"It's great," she said, meaning it. "I just got a new client that reminds me so much of dad." Her throat closed when she said it, realizing for the first time how much Sean Hawthorne reminded her of her own father.

"Oh, really?"

Holland hated how her mother's voice brightened. "Yeah, he just had a hip fracture, and I'm in charge of his physical therapy." She tried not to let her mind go back to her father's physical therapy and her complete inability to help him.

But her brain did it anyway, calling up the memories that always seemed so fresh, so close to the surface, so loud when they labeled her a failure.

"That's great, hon," her mom said, almost silencing the memories. "I'm calling to let you know that Lisa is set to have the baby any day now."

Emotion clogged Holland's throat. She wasn't the only

one who'd walked too close to the edge after her father's death. At least she'd only chosen the wrong man to date. But Lisa had chosen the wrong man and then gotten pregnant. When the wrong guy had bailed, Lisa had been left with a baby bump and a really hard decision.

"What's she going to do?" Holland asked. The thought of having a niece or a nephew made Holland feel fuzzy and warm, but Lisa hadn't learned the sex of the baby. She'd been waffling back and forth between keeping the baby and putting it up for adoption. At only twenty-three-years-old, her decision was life-changing.

"She's not sure," her mom said with a sigh. "I'm trying not to influence her."

Her mother wanted Lisa to put the baby up for adoption, give a couple the opportunity to be parents who couldn't have children of their own. Holland knew her mother was worn out, and while she'd love grandchildren, she didn't want to be the primary caregiver for the baby.

"I'll text her," Holland said. "See how she's feeling." Lisa always told Holland more than she told her mother. At least more of the truth. "How's Brenda?" Holland barely squeezed the name out of her throat.

She hadn't spoken to Brenda since the day she'd left town. In fact, Brenda and Jordan were the reason Holland had packed everything she owned and traveled four hundred miles to Gold Valley.

She still couldn't believe Jordan had stuck around for so long, and Holland was starting to wonder if he had an ulterior motive.

Of course he does, she thought as her mom said Brenda was doing just fine. Almost done with her makeup artistry program. She'd started it a year ago, had done Holland's makeup for her first date with Jordan, but still hadn't finished. She just couldn't seem to "find the time" to finish the training and get a job.

But she had time to date Jordan's brother while Holland dated Jordan. Time to mess around behind Holland's back. Time to break up with the brother and start dating Jordan—the very next day after Holland had ended things with him.

It was all a tangled mess Holland didn't want to get caught up in again. Whenever she allowed herself to delve into those months, she ended up feeling insecure and unhappy. She spiraled down into a deep, dark place she didn't like visiting.

She inhaled and focused on what her mother was saying. She'd moved on from Brenda and was talking about her book club, thankfully. Holland loved her mother and wanted to support her, so she re-engaged in the conversation, pushing Brenda and Jordan and everything that had brought her to Gold Valley out of her mind.

She was happy to be here, was thriving here, and she didn't see any sense in looking backward.

Lucy perked up from where she'd settled at Holland's feet. A single bark echoed throughout her room, and Holland turned toward the doorway. "I gotta go, Mom," she said, her heart pounding. Thundering. Galloping.

"Who is it, girl?" she asked the dog as Holland stood and ran her fingers through her short hair. *Please let it be Elliott.*

Lucy wagged her tail as she trotted down the hall and toward the front door. Holland followed somewhat slower, though Gold Valley had to be the safest town on the planet. She peered through the peephole and sure enough, a man wearing a black cowboy hat stood on the front porch, facing the street. Elliott swung back to the door and lifted his hand to knock again, a concerned expression on his face.

Holland whipped the door open, almost getting hit in the face as Elliott moved to knock. "Oh!" She jumped back at the same time Lucy mobbed Elliott.

He chuckled as he made space for the sheep-labradoodle on the front porch and scrubbed behind her ears. "Look at you. What's your name?" He crouched down and let Lucy lick his ears, dislodging his cowboy hat completely as he laughed.

The sight of him becoming friends with Lucy—who as a rule didn't like anyone—made Holland like him even more. His sandy blond hair was clipped short and he looked more youthful without the hat. Just as good-looking. Just as sexy.

He straightened and looked at her. "What kind of dog is this?"

"Labradoodle," Holland managed to say. "Lucy, come on. Leave him alone." Of course, Lucy ignored her, and Holland ended up pulling the dog back into the house by her collar. "Let me just grab my purse." She flashed him a stressed smile. "You can come in."

He stepped into the house, immediately changing the space. Holland would never be able to walk through that door without seeing him framed there, glancing around and nodding appreciatively.

"Where's Cecil?" he asked.

"He works nights sometimes." Holland took a deep breath and lifted her purse from the kitchen counter. "Tonight is one of those nights."

"Sorry for just droppin' by," Elliott said. "I never got your number, and we never set plans." His voice strummed a chord somewhere in her soul, getting louder as he approached her.

She turned to find him only a step behind her. A smile formed on his face, completely knocking down all her defenses.

Don't kiss him! she screamed at herself. Then she really would have kissed him before the first date.

"I've been thinkin' about you all day," he said, his fingers flirting with hers, brushing tip to tip and sending sparks all the way through her.

"Oh yeah?" Holland arched toward him, latching onto his fingers completely now that he'd initiated contact. She hadn't been out of the dating scene for so long that she didn't know how to flirt.

"Yeah." Elliott grinned down at her and lifted one hand to the back of her head. His fingers traced the short, shaved hair along the nape of her neck, up and around to her ear. She closed her eyes, her breath shuddering out of her body.

"You're...I don't really know what's goin' on here," Elliott said. "I hardly know you, but I really like you."

"Mm." Holland liked the sound of his voice in her ears, the tender way his thumb and forefinger caressed her earlobe. If he didn't kiss her in the next five seconds, Holland thought she'd combust for sure.

"You shave your hair?" he asked, his breath cascading over her cheek and throat.

"Yeah," she said. "It's so thick, and this way, it lies flat." She opened her eyes, surprised at how close he was and yet he hadn't kissed her yet.

She breathed in the spicy, masculine scent of his skin, her hands automatically going up to steal strength from his shoulders. "Are you going to kiss me soon?" she whispered.

He jerked the teensiest bit and pulled back. Their eyes met, fireworks shooting through his. "You want me to?"

"Well, you have to finish what you started last night." She smiled up at him in what she hoped was an invitational way. "I've been thinking about *that* all day, I'll have you know."

"My boss told me I couldn't kiss you before the date."

"My cousin said the same thing."

His eyes dropped to her mouth, and he brought her half a step closer to him. "This is weird, right? How we feel about each other?"

"It's new for me," she admitted. "But maybe it's not weird. Maybe it's just…." She didn't know how to finish, so she let her eyes drift halfway closed, hoping he'd erase the distance between them.

He did, and the moment his mouth fully touched hers, Holland knew the right word to complete her sentence.

Different.

New.

Exciting.

But definitely not weird.

Elliott didn't care what he'd have to confess to Ty that night when he got back to the ranch. Kissing Holland was at least a hundred times better in real life than what he'd imagined. She kissed him back, her mouth moving quite in sync with his, her fingers in his hair, her body pressed right up against his.

He felt a hunger inside him that had nothing to do with food and everything to do with Holland, so he kissed her until she pulled away. And he still wanted more.

"Should we go eat?" she asked.

"Yeah," he said dumbly, unsure if he could actually form more words than that. His head felt light while his legs felt heavy, but he managed to follow her out the front door. She wore a pair of black shorts that barely reached her mid-thigh and a billowy blouse the color of pink lemonade. He liked the shape of her, the straps on her black sandals, the way she glanced over her shoulder with a sly smile to see if he was following her.

He was. And he had the strangest sensation that he'd go wherever she wanted him to go.

"What do you like?" he asked as she approached his truck. He opened the passenger door for her and put his hand on her waist as she boosted herself into the cab.

He couldn't believe she let him. Couldn't believe that in the time it took for him to circle the truck, she'd slid across the seat, barely leaving any room for him.

"You like burgers," she said. "What about steak?"

"Is there a cowboy alive who doesn't like steak?" He cut her a glance. "Do *you* like steak?"

"I've eaten it before."

"So that's a no." The chemistry between them crackled, and Elliott wondered if this was the feeling Archer had described. He didn't know, and he wasn't sure he cared. He liked this buzz, the feathery touch of Holland's hand in his, the scent of oranges and lilacs that streamed from her.

"What about pizza?" he asked.

"What about Italian?" she countered.

He didn't really care, so he said, "I like Italian," and steered the truck toward downtown. "So we've established you have a bad ex-boyfriend," he said. "What about your family?"

Holland groaned, and Elliott glanced at her. "Okay, so the family's off-limits too." He wanted to know the good, the bad, and the ugly, but he understood it wasn't easy to talk about.

"My last boyfriend was so serious that I wore a diamond." She pulled in a breath in tandem with Elliott, who hadn't expected her to say that.

He had been thinking about her all day—most of last night too. But he hadn't expected her to be engaged.

"We'd only been together for about six months. It was all wrong. He was wrong for me; I was wrong for him. The engagement was wrong. I knew it; he knew it."

Elliott didn't know what to say, so he just nodded and kept driving.

"I broke things off when I found out he was two-timing me with my sister. They're still together."

Shock traveled through Elliott like a tidal wave. "Wow." He swallowed, trying to find the right words to comfort Holland. All he could come up with was, "I see why you left, and why family is off-limits."

"My mom is great," she said.

"No dad?"

Her pain radiated through the cab, and Elliott cursed himself for asking so insensitively. "Sorry, Holland. Off-limits means off-limits."

"He passed away," she said. "Two years ago. None of us handled it well. I started dating Jordan, and Brenda, the sister he cheated with, dated his brother. And Lisa, my youngest sister is having a baby in a few days. The father is out of the picture. So." She gave a laugh that was probably meant to be light, but sounded weighed down with a million reasons why she'd left her hometown.

"Where is your family?" he asked.

"Idaho Falls."

"Are you going to go visit when your sister has the baby?"

She exhaled and pulled out her phone. "No, she's not even sure she's going to keep it." She removed her hand from his, saying, "Sorry, I told my mom I'd text her. After this, I'll put my phone away."

"It's fine," Elliott said, but he appreciated that she understood the importance of being with people when she was with people. He glanced down at her phone and found a picture of a wedding dress.

Surprise flowed with fear through him. *Don't ask*, he told himself. *Do not ask right now.*

He pressed his lips together and managed to keep the words inside his mouth. She stuffed the phone back into her purse and cuddled into his side. "So tell me about you."

"Not much to tell, honestly," he said. "Youngest of four brothers, as I'm sure you gathered from the dozens of family photos at my parents' house."

"Yep."

"Everyone is married except for me. I'm almost thirty, and I've been working at Horseshoe Home for a decade now." He couldn't believe his life could be boiled down to so few words. He worried he wouldn't be exciting enough for Holland.

"And you like dogs," she said.

"And horses," he said. "And even chickens."

"Cows?"

"Aw, they're stubborn as heck, but yeah. They keep my

bills paid, so I guess I like cows too." He gave her a brilliant smile that caused her face to light up. He hoped he could do that again, and he squeezed her fingers before lifting them to his lips.

"And you like dogs," he said.

"But not horses, chickens, or cows," she said.

"Fair enough." He pulled into the parking lot at Mama Mia's and took the truck out of gear. "You like your job?"

"I *love* my job."

He gazed at her, his thoughts swirling. Her eyes softened the longer he looked at her, and he wanted to kiss her again. Instead, he said, "I'm glad you moved to Gold Valley," and opened the door.

She slid out after him, and he took her hand in his. He talked about the dogs out on the ranch, and she told him about Lucy's insecurities as they went inside the restaurant. It wasn't a weekend, and it was almost eight o'clock, so getting a table wasn't a problem.

Elliott couldn't seem to see beyond Holland, because he barely heard the man who said, "Elliott?" until he'd said it twice.

Then he turned toward his brother, who scanned Elliott and Holland from head to toe, his gaze landing on their joined hands.

"What are you two doing here?" He rose from his table, setting his napkin back on the table while his wife watched.

"We're…." Elliott glanced at Holland. "Going to dinner," he finished.

"Like, as a date?"

"No—" Holland started, trying to pull her hand away.

But Elliott held onto her. Tugged her closer even. "Yes," he said. "Like as a date."

Joel advanced one step that crowded Elliott though he was still several paces away. "She's Dad's physical therapist."

"So what?" Elliott hadn't felt anything for a woman in five years. He wasn't letting go of this magic because she worked with his father.

"She—it's…unprofessional." Joel's eyes flicked to Holland's.

"It's fine," Elliott said. "We're not doing anything wrong by going to dinner."

Demmie stood. "Let it go, Joel," she said quietly, shooting a glance in Elliott's direction. She'd probably paid more attention over the past five years, had seen Elliott's struggles in the dating arena. She put her hand on Joel's arm and nudged him toward the exit. "Have fun, you two." She flashed a quick smile before grabbing her purse and following Joel out.

The mood had definitely been dampened, and Elliott sat across from Holland, unable to look at her fully. A band of pressure sat around his lungs, making it hard to get a proper breath.

"He might be right," she said, which finally pulled Elliott's eyes to hers.

"He's not right."

"I don't normally date my patients."

"I'm not your patient." He gazed at her evenly, some of that spark between them returning.

"It could be viewed as unprofessional." She tucked her hair behind her ear, revealing some of that sexy shaved part. He was surprised how much he liked her non-traditional hairstyle. He'd never dated someone with hair color so obviously from a bottle, and a style so unique.

"By who?" he challenged. "My ultra-conservative brother?"

"What will your parents think?" She gave some of his fire right back to him, something he also appreciated.

"My mother will probably start crying," he said. Her face fell. "Because she's been praying for me to meet a woman for about five years." He returned his attention to the menu, though he already knew what he wanted. He just didn't want Holland to see the hurt streaming from his eyes the way it had infected his voice.

"Five years, huh?"

"Been on a lot of first dates," he said.

"No wonder this is going so well." The playful tease in her voice made the tension in his muscles ease. "And no wonder you cut straight to the kiss. I mean, if it's not good, at least you know up front, right?"

He looked at her, trying to figure out if she was joking, or hurt, or something else. "I haven't kissed a woman in a long time."

"No?" She tucked that hair that hadn't moved. "Well, that's surprising."

"Why?"

She closed her menu and leaned her elbows on it, inching closer to him. He found himself tilting toward her too. "Because you're really good at it for being out of practice." The teasing sparkle in her eyes sent fireworks through his system.

"I don't normally do that before a first date," he said. "Or after it. Honest."

She leaned back and glanced up as the waitress approached with water glasses. "I believe you."

They ordered, and she lifted her water glass to her lips and sipped. Elliott tracked her every move, his gaze lingering on those very kissable lips.

"And Elliott, I hope you break the mold again after our date tonight." She giggled and Elliott's pulse skyrocketed. He definitely wanted to kiss her again, even if someone viewed it as unprofessional.

———

Ty waited on the top step of Elliott's front porch. Archer was with him, which sent another bolt of surprise through Elliott.

"You're back," he said to his old cabin mate. He let out a low groan as he sat down beside Archer. "How was the honeymoon?"

"Great," Archer said, all the elaboration Elliott would get. "How was your date?"

"Great," Elliott said. He knew why Ty and Archer were here, waiting for him. And he knew he'd tell them about the kiss with Holland. He'd always detailed his dating escapades. Difference here was that this was actually a good date. No weird stories. No tube tops. Nothing that had scared him off—except for his own strong feelings.

"You like her," Ty said.

"Yeah," Elliott agreed.

"So will there be a second date?" Archer asked.

"Tomorrow." A smile curved Elliott's mouth. He felt like he'd achieved his personal best in a race or a video game. He hadn't made it to a second date in years.

"So you *really* like her," Ty said.

"Kissed her," Elliott said. "So I guess I really like her."

Archer whistled at the same time Ty whooped. "A kiss on the first date," Archer said. "Wow."

"It was actually before," Elliott said, a giddiness prancing through him that felt silly. "And during. And after." The pressure of her mouth against his was almost palpable, the taste of her chocolate dessert still on his tongue.

"You really don't mess around," Ty said.

"There's something about her," Elliott said. "It's like she's…." He let his voice trail off, because uttering the words "my soul mate" to these two other rough and tough cowboys felt stupid.

But Elliott wondered if she really was his soul mate. If such a thing even existed.

CHAPTER 6

*D*o you want to sit by me at church tomorrow?

Elliott's question wafted around in Holland's head like a cobweb. He had her pressed against the front door, his mouth tracing a pattern on her neck and ears she really liked.

She couldn't believe she'd met him three days ago. She felt like she'd known him for three years, that he'd taken twelve months to ask her out. Taken her on dozens of dates before kissing her. And that they were just now advancing to the next stage.

But it had all happened in seventy-two hours.

Still, she heard herself say, "Sure, church tomorrow," and she felt Elliott's lips curve upward as he smiled against her throat. He pulled back, leaving her cold and craving more of his kisses.

"Want me to come pick you up, or can we meet there?"

"I usually go with Cecil," she said. "So we can meet, especially since the church is almost at the mouth of the canyon. No reason for you to come all the way over here and then go back."

He touched the tip of his nose to hers. "Great, I'll see you then." He went down the steps backward, that delicious smile making his face as close to perfection as Holland thought possible. She pressed one palm against her pulse as he sauntered back to his truck and got in. He waved as he drove away, and Holland exhaled, trying to organize her thoughts and emotions.

An almost impossible task.

Cecil yanked open the door, causing her to yelp as she nearly fell backward into the house. "What are you doing out here, young lady?" he asked. He glanced up at the dark light bulb. "And why isn't this working?" He flipped the switch several times.

"I don't know," she fibbed, not wanting to tell him that Elliott had reached up with his bare hand and loosened the bulb enough to leave them in darkness. Leave them to be able to smooch without the prying eyes of the neighborhood—of Cecil.

Holland ducked past her cousin without meeting his eye. "Did you make any of that orange hot chocolate?"

"You know I did. You've been standing out on the porch smelling it for ten minutes." He followed her into the kitchen.

Holland had been caught, and she knew it. She poured herself a cup of the fruity-chocolatey drink and glanced at him. "Do you believe in love at first sight?"

Cecil's normal quick wit and rapid comebacks didn't happen. He sighed as he sat at the bar, and she had her answer.

"I just feel…something for him that doesn't make sense." She curled her fingers around her mug. "From the very moment he walked through that doorway, I—I've only been able to see him. Think about him. He's kind, faithful, hardworking, funny. He helps his parents. He—he—he's wonderful."

And Holland truly believed he was. Tonight, they'd simply picked up street waffles from the food truck and wandered the streets of Gold Valley. He'd detailed memories from his childhood, with his brothers, in the park, at the waterfalls, all of it.

She hadn't said a whole lot more about her family, but he hadn't pushed her. He'd said he understood messy, and that they'd deal with her sisters as they had to.

They.

She'd liked the sound of that single word so much she hadn't been able to articulate much for several minutes.

He spoke like they had a long future together, and Holland had to admit she'd started thinking the same way. After only three days.

"I feel slightly insane," she admitted to Cecil. "He asked me to sit with him at church tomorrow."

A panicked look crossed Cecil's face, but he covered it quickly. "That's great, Holland."

"You'll still sit by me, right?"

"Why would I? I don't need that third wheel status too. Divorced is bad enough."

"Oh, come on." She sipped her hot chocolate, enjoying the citrusy tang of the orange. "No one's judging you for being divorced." Especially since his ex-wife had gone off the deep end and left town without a word to anyone. She still hadn't come back to Gold Valley, and Cecil had boxed up everything of his ex's and put it in a storage unit.

"And I saw Lena Lopez eying you last week."

"She was not." But a hopeful glint entered his eyes.

"She was," Holland said. "In the foyer. She was leaning into the doorway, and smiling at you." Holland grinned and pressed into the counter as if reenacting the encounter from last week. "You should talk to her tomorrow. Maybe consider asking her out."

"Oh, I've considered it," Cecil muttered.

———

The simple sight of Elliott Hawthorne standing on the sidewalk outside the church, wearing a pair of black slacks, a sky blue shirt, and a yellow and blue striped tie with that black cowboy hat was enough to send Holland's pulse into the stratosphere.

She nearly squealed and skipped over to him, but kept her step even lest she break a leg in the heels she'd chosen to wear. Shiny black, they matched the black pencil skirt and the black and white polka dotted blouse.

Elliott saw her from dozens of feet away, and his gaze

devoured her as she came nearer. "You remember Cecil," she said, indicating her cousin beside her.

"Of course." Elliott extended his hand for Cecil to shake. "You're a few years older than me. Were you in Ray's class?"

"Between him and Donny," Cecil said, shaking Elliott's hand with a smile.

"He's sitting with us," Holland said as she laced her hand through Elliott's elbow. "He's got his eye on Lena Lopez."

"Holland," Cecil said in a warning voice.

"Oh, Lena," Elliott said. "I went out with her last summer. She adores yellow roses." He tapped the brim of his cowboy hat. "You could start there, and be in a great position to get that date." He stepped toward the front doors, and suddenly Cecil was his shadow.

"You went out with her?"

"Once." Elliott glanced at Holland. "I went on a lot of first dates."

"Why no second date?" Cecil asked.

"She wasn't my type."

"Do you think I'm her type?"

Elliott paused and looked at Cecil. "I have no idea, man." He chuckled. "I don't even know what my type is. I just knew there wasn't a spark there."

"Not a spark," Cecil said thoughtfully, entering the church first.

Holland followed Elliott inside and claimed his hand again. "So there are sparks between us?"

"Entire firework shows," he whispered as they went into

the chapel and slid onto a bench. He lifted his arm and tucked her into his side. "You can't feel it?"

Oh, she could feel it. She put her hand on his knee and squeezed, causing his muscles to tense and him to duck his head close to her ear.

"So you do feel it." He chuckled as the pastor got up and started the sermon.

Holland tried to listen, but it was almost impossible when everything she looked at was overlaid in lace and diamonds. She'd spent more time pinning designer wedding dresses and different cuts of diamonds on her Pinterest board in the last twenty-four hours than she had in the entire time she'd been engaged.

The urge to pull out her phone and search through the options for party favors nearly consumed her, but she kept her device out of sight. She didn't want Elliott to get spooked by her ravenous wedding thoughts—which were ridiculous really.

She'd known the man for four days.

Her phone buzzed but still she didn't pull it out. The preacher spoke about standing for what was right in this new day and age, and she tried to focus on the words. But her phone vibrated again.

Could be Lisa, she thought, which prompted her to pull the phone out from under her leg.

Her mother had texted. *Lisa just went into labor. She told me she's going to put the baby up for adoption.*

Holland's heart didn't know if it should rejoice or droop in sadness. She knew Lisa would be devastated to let the baby go, but she also believed that baby deserved a family with a mother and a father.

Holland had texted just before her Italian meal with Elliott that Lisa needed to think about the child more than herself.

No judgment, she'd sent. *But do what's best for that baby.*

Her mother's next message said, *She wants you here. Can you come?*

This time, Holland's heart knew exactly what to do, and it sank all the way into her shoes.

"You gonna go?" Elliott whispered, his mouth so close to her earlobe that his bottom lip caught against the edge of her ear.

She shivered, pure delight flowing through her. It didn't mix well with the desperation firing through her, screaming at her to stay in Gold Valley. She'd warned her mother she might not come back to Idaho Falls very often. Her mom had seemed understanding at the time. And if she went to see Lisa, she'd have to see Brenda. And wherever Brenda was, Jordan was sure to be.

So many ripples, she thought.

If she didn't go, what would that do to Lisa?

Let me talk to my boss, she texted to her mother. Then she immediately started praying that Kevin would say he simply couldn't spare her.

———

Holland put another pair of shorts in her suitcase, her mood worsening by the moment. Elliott had dropped her off, kissed her, and gone back up to the ranch. Reluctantly, sure, which buoyed Holland's spirits for about two seconds before she remembered that Kevin had been *so* understanding. So much like, "Take as much time as you need."

Holland didn't want to take any time. But she couldn't see how she could get out of going.

I know you don't want to come, her mom had texted while Holland waited out the rest of the sermon. While she texted Kevin. *But Lisa really wants you here. She needs someone strong to help her through this.*

Holland didn't feel strong. And she'd feel even weaker as soon as she crossed into Idaho Falls.

It took seven and a half hours to drive to Idaho Falls. If she could delay just a little longer, she'd get there closer to midnight. She'd buy herself until morning before she had to see anyone but her mom.

Maybe Brenda would've already been to the hospital to visit. Maybe Holland wouldn't have to see her or Jordan. Maybe, maybe, maybe.

She sighed as she went to gather her toiletries. *Give me patience to deal with my sisters,* she prayed, finishing her packing and heaving the suitcase off her bed.

"Well, I'm off," she said to Cecil, who sat at the kitchen table with a plate of toast and a bowl of beef stew in front of him.

He abandoned his food and stood, taking her suitcase from her. "I'm sorry, Holland," he said.

"It's okay," she said, following him out to her car.

"It's not." He put the suitcase in the trunk. "It would be like me going to meet Serene. It's absolutely not okay." He grabbed her and pulled her into a hug. "Don't let them hurt you again, okay?"

Holland knew exactly who he was talking about—Brenda and Jordan—and she nodded, her tears threatening to overflow from the kindness of her cousin.

Then she got in her car and set it on a course south, back toward the one place she never wanted to go again.

Her legs felt numb and she had to go to the bathroom something urgent by the time she pulled into her mother's driveway. Only a dim light shone from somewhere within the house, and her mom's car wasn't in the garage.

She called, "Mom?" as she entered, but no one answered. The house was empty, and Holland sent a prayer of gratitude heavenward for the opportunity to be here alone, even if only for a few minutes.

Half an hour later, her mom entered the house looking tired and worn. "Sweetheart," she said as Holland rose from the couch where she'd been texting Elliott.

"Mom." A fierce rush of love and missing filled Holland as she hugged her mother. "How's Lisa?"

"Fine."

"The baby?"

"It was a healthy baby boy. She didn't even hold him." Emotion choked her mother's voice, and Holland finally allowed her tears to overflow.

Her mom released Holland and moved into the kitchen

where Holland had made coffee. "I know it's silly, because I've been pushing her toward adoption since the day we found out she was pregnant." She poured a cup of coffee and added a heaping spoonful of sugar to it. "It's harder than I thought it would be. That's *my* grandchild."

"I know." Holland put her hand on her mom's shoulder. "Did you get to meet the couple?"

She nodded as she sipped. "Lisa and I chose them together. They were so emotional, so grateful, so wonderful. Lisa didn't want to see them." She exhaled and Holland led her to the couch so she could rest. "I met with them for a few minutes in the waiting room."

Holland didn't know what to say to comfort her mom, to drive away the worry lines around her eyes.

"So tell me something good," her mom said. "How's Gold Valley? Maybe I should come visit my sister."

"You should," Holland said. "Aunt Wendy would like that, and you need a break from…everything."

Her mom managed a weak smile and patted Holland's knee. "Anything new with you?"

Holland's mind spun, and she took a moment to wipe her eyes dry. Should she tell her mother about Elliott? It certainly was "something good" for Holland, but she wasn't sure if her mom would view it the same way. After cuddling with Elliott in church today, she was actually surprised Aunt Wendy hadn't already texted her sister about the relationship.

"I met a man," Holland said in measured beats. "His

name's Elliott, and he's a cowboy at a ranch up the canyon from town."

"Hmm, a cowboy." Her mom's eyes sparkled with excitement.

"He's great," Holland said.

"How long have you known him?"

"Not long," Holland hedged. She definitely didn't want to tell her mom about the before-the-first-date kiss.

"Did you know your father worked at a ranch for a few years?"

Holland swung her gaze to her mother's. "No." She smiled and giggled. "He did?"

"Three years, I think. Then we met, and I told him I wasn't keen on marrying a cowboy. He quit the next day and started at the vocational school within the month." A fond look crossed her face, and she stared past Holland, almost as if she could see a younger version of her husband, experience that time in her life again.

"I like my cowboy," Holland said.

"It's not an easy life," her mom said.

"I know that." But Holland didn't, not really. She knew Elliott carried a measure of exhaustion with him, but she had no idea what he actually did to become that tired. "Mom, how long did you know Dad before you knew he was the one for you?"

A thoughtful look crossed her mom's face. "I knew really early. A few weeks, probably. That's why I mentioned the part about the cowboy to him." She grinned and smoothed her hair down. "When he quit and started school, I knew he felt that same powerful something between us."

A week ago, Holland wouldn't have understood what that "powerful something" was. But she did now. A healthy dose of fear flowed through her.

Sure, she'd spent years planning her dream wedding, looking at dresses, imagining what her bridesmaids would wear. Nowhere had her visions included a black cowboy hat, but now that was all she could see.

"Well, let's get to bed." Her mom exhaled heavily as she stood. "We'll have to get back to the hospital in the morning." She set her coffee mug on the kitchen counter, and Holland followed her down the hall to the guest bedroom where she'd already stored her suitcase.

She hugged her mom goodnight and closed the door behind her, leaning into it, thoughts of a country cowboy wedding parading through her mind. It was late, and Elliott had likely gone to bed. He'd said she'd woken him when she'd found herself home alone and had texted him.

He had an early morning, but Holland couldn't help experimenting with the wording of a text. *I love you, Elliott.*

She stared at the letters, her tears now borne from happiness instead of sorrow. She dropped her thumb to erase the sentiment. It was too soon to say such things, and they shouldn't be sent in a text anyway.

The blue conversation bubble shot above the area where she typed, and her heart seized.

Instead of deleting the message, she'd *sent it.* All four words, just gone into the textosphere.

And she couldn't unsend them.

65

CHAPTER 7

Elliott woke to the sound of pounding on his cabin door. He bolted upright in bed and worked to free his feet from the blanket. He slept in gym shorts and nothing else, so he took a moment to grab a T-shirt from the floor on his way to the front door.

He wrenched the door open to find six cowboys standing there, wide smiles on their faces. Ty stood in the front, with Jace—the owner of the ranch—right beside him.

"What's goin' on?" Elliott asked, still trying to thread one arm through his shirt the right way. He looked at Archer, who surely had to get up before the sun to be standing on this porch at this hour. "Arch?"

"We're here to offer you the job of general controller," Jace said. "Ty thinks you're the man for the job. Caleb, who's done it in a pinch, said so too." He looked at Caleb, who ran the agricultural side of the ranch.

Confusion mingled with surprise and a hint of pride.

"The general controller? I didn't even know Nels was leaving." He glanced at the older cowboy who'd been sitting behind the desk in the administration lodge for years.

"I just found out yesterday too," Jace said, following Elliott's gaze to Nels. "Retiring, and he wants to do it soon."

"My wife is ready to get that RV and travel the country," Nels said. "I think you'd be great behind the desk, Elliott."

"So what do you say?" Ty asked. "It's primarily desk work, but the hours are better."

"You'll still be on the weekend chore rotation," Jace added.

"And you'll have to deal with the public more," Archer added.

Elliott wasn't deterred by any of that. He had a couple of questions, but he didn't want the committee on his porch to hear his selfish thoughts. He could ask Ty in private. Or Jace.

"You'd have more time for Holland," Archer said. "Or, you know, Precious."

Both, Elliott thought. He wanted to know if he'd make more money and if he'd have to share a cabin. Nels didn't live on the ranch—maybe Elliott wouldn't be able to stay.

Committee or not, he needed to know. "Terms?" he asked.

"It's better pay," Jace said. "And since you're single, you can stay in your cabin."

He leaned against the doorway. "What if I find myself not single?"

"Told ya it was serious," Archer said, glancing at Ty.

"He's been dating her for a few days," the foreman shot back.

"Boys," Jace said. "Don't hound the man." He looked back at Elliott. "If you get married, we'd have to evaluate our housing. I've got a new man coming next week, and I was going to put him up with you."

The air left Elliott's lungs. Of course Jace wouldn't let Elliott live alone, not when there were new cowboys that needed housing. "What's his name?"

"Gordon Escariot," Jace said.

Didn't sound like a cowboy name at all, but Elliott kept that thought to himself. "I'll take the general controller job."

Archer's face burst into a smile. Nels's did too. "Great," the older man said. "So you'll be working with me for the next couple of weeks, and then you'll be ready to take over."

The cowboys disbanded one by one until only Ty remained. He hooked his arm over Elliott's shoulders and went into the cabin with him, asking, "You got any coffee on?"

"It's five-thirty in the morning. I wasn't even going to get up for another hour." He moved into the kitchen and started filling the coffee pot. "Is that how you do things around here? Bust down cabin doors early in the morning?"

"It was Archer's idea." Ty grinned like it was a great idea, and Elliott rolled his eyes. "So you and Holland really are serious, huh?"

"I suppose," he said, though he knew they were. Knew he didn't go around kissing women the very first night he'd met them. Knew there was something strong between them that had burst into existence the first time he'd seen her. Knew she felt the same about him.

Ty scoffed. "You suppose. You lookin' at rings yet?"

Elliott thought about the wedding things he'd seen on Holland's phone at church yesterday. "I barely know her mom's name."

"You kissed the woman the very night you met her."

"That wasn't a kiss." Elliott enjoyed the percolating sound of the coffee pot getting ready to produce the liquid caffeine he needed to make it through days that started this early. He rolled his eyes at Ty, but the idea of looking for a diamond ring for Holland plagued him.

Stuck with him after Ty left with a knowing smile on his face. Tantalized him as he pulled up a chair to Nels's desk and took notes on what the general controller did. Enthralled him as he walked back to his place for lunch.

His phone was ringing when he entered the cabin, and he immediately tried to think of the last time he'd seen it. The sound came from his bedroom, and Elliott realized he'd left it there that morning after his rude awakening.

The light blinked from the dresser, and Holland's face sat on the screen. He swiped it on at the last second with a "Hey, Holland."

"Elliott," she sounded relieved.

"You okay?" he asked.

"I've called a couple of times."

"I left my phone at the cabin," he said. "Because I got a new job, and I was a little excited this morning."

"You got a new job?" she asked.

"Yeah, Jace just promoted me to general controller." He tried not to sound so proud of himself, but he couldn't help it. "More money. Less outdoor work. Shorter hours."

She wore a smile in her voice when she said, "That sounds great, Elliott."

"It is great." He went into the kitchen in search of bread and peanut butter. "So, tell me how everything went with your sister."

"Lisa is great," she said. "She's recovering well, and she should be able to go home later today even."

"Wow, that soon?"

"She had the baby in the morning yesterday, so it'll have been almost two full days." She sighed. "I saw Brenda and Jordan from down the hall, and I ducked in here to call you." Her voice dropped with every word she said. "I just can't face them alone. My mom went down to the cafeteria to get lunch."

"So they really are still together." Elliott wasn't really asking.

"I guess so." She sighed. "So you haven't looked at your texts yet?"

"Six cowboys nearly collapsed my house at five-thirty this morning to ask me about the new job," he said. "So, no, I haven't looked at my phone at all today."

"Oh, um."

Elliott waited for her to say what she needed to say. She'd never seemed to have a problem telling him things. She'd been open about her relationship with Jordan, emotional when she detailed her dad's quick demise due to colon cancer, enthusiastic when she spoke of her college training and her physical therapy job.

"Holland?" he asked.

"I sent you something last night," she blurted. "It was an accident, and I didn't mean to send it. I was just sort of…I don't know what."

"Well, what did it say?"

"Oh, I can't say it out loud."

"You sent me something you can't say out loud?" Elliott smiled out the window at the horizon. "Wow, Holland. I can't wait to look at it."

"No, you should just delete it."

He couldn't seem to get his knife spreading peanut butter again. "I'm not gonna do that," he said. "I'm totally intrigued."

She exhaled like he was a petulant toddler, which elicited a laugh from Elliott. He got the sandwich made as she said, "Fine, but just know it was an accident."

"All righty." He took a bite of his sandwich and chewed.

"I have to go. I'm sure Brenda will have me paged soon."

His heart went out to her. "Hang in there, beautiful. Just a few hours, right?"

"I'm hoping for six thirty-minute increments."

"And then you'll call me again," he said. "So I'll be counting down the increments too." He'd told her about his thirty-minute increment life, and she hadn't made fun of him. Hadn't asked why he had to segment his life in order to live it.

And now that he had her and a new job, he wondered if he really needed to partition his life so much.

He remembered that he had a new cabin mate coming next week, but living week by week was better than half-hour by half-hour.

"Okay, I'll call you soon," she said.

"Sounds good, Holland. Love you, bye." He hung up and picked up his sandwich to take another bite, his voice rebounding around inside his head.

Love you, bye.

Love you, bye?

He froze mid-chew. Had he really just told her he loved her? He groaned as he put his forehead on the table, the words still reverberating through his ears.

So it was a slip. It was what he said to his mother when she called. It was meaningless.

He lifted his head, his appetite gone as he flipped over his phone to check her text. He honestly had no idea what she could've sent that she couldn't say out loud.

He only had one text from her. Two missed calls, but one text.

I love you, Elliott.

His breath left his body. Those four words weren't a *Love you, bye* slip. They were life-changing. They were something deliberate she'd thumbed out and then sent.

"She said it was an accident," he said to the partially eaten peanut butter sandwich. But why would she have typed such a message at all? How was *that* an accident?

He pushed away from the kitchen table, abandoning his sandwich but taking his phone with him.

Fear filled him. Starting with his father's accident, he felt like his whole life had been turned upside down. Five days. He'd met Holland five days ago. Was it insane to love her so quickly?

It was definitely pure insanity for her to love him.

Elliott burst from the containing walls of his cabin and headed for the stables. He didn't care that he had a full afternoon of general controlling ahead of him. He needed to take Precious up into the mountains and figure things out.

Figure out why he thought he wasn't loveable.

Figure out how Holland could possibly have made a mistake with those particular words.

CHAPTER 8

*L*ove you, bye.

Anxiety ate a hole through Holland. It had been gnawing since she'd sent that text the previous evening. She wasn't sure how she'd fallen asleep at all, but she had.

And now she had to face her sister knowing that Elliott had seen her accidental text. What would he think? Would he call her back right away? And what had he meant by *Love you, bye?*

It was said so flippantly, Holland didn't think he even knew he'd said it. He didn't really love her—and she didn't want him to say it like that if he did. She really wanted him to call her back, and she checked her phone to make sure she had service in this wing of the hospital. She did. Her phone didn't ring.

At least her mom had caught her in the hall and given

her one of the paper bags full of food. "We can really eat this in Lisa's room?" Holland asked.

"Yep. I even asked the nurse." Her mom slid her a glance. "Have you seen Brenda yet?"

"Yes." Holland sighed. "I ducked into a closet so I wouldn't have to face her and Jordan alone." Holland didn't want to see them at all. Ever. Just thinking about them set her back in her progress toward a happier, healthier future.

Hang in there. Elliott's encouraging words rang through her mind. *Thirty minutes,* she told herself. Just get through the next thirty minutes.

"Lisa and I will be your buffer."

"I'm still gonna have to talk to them," Holland said as she pushed the button to enter the maternity ward.

"Lisa will tell them to behave," her mom said. "She pretty much laid down the law for Brenda's visit."

"She did?" Holland thought of her youngest sister, usually the shy one half a step behind everyone else.

"She did. She said she would already be going through a lot of turmoil, and she didn't want Brenda causing problems." They approached Lisa's room, and Holland's steps slowed automatically.

Her mom entered first, and Holland slipped in behind her. "Food's here," her mom said, and Brenda turned from Lisa's bedside, a wide smile on her face.

Holland stepped behind her mom and put her bag of food on the counter. Jordan lingered across the small hospital room, the bed between them, which was just fine with Holland. He met her eye and looked away quickly, a small triumph for her.

"Burgers for everyone," Mom said. "Even you, Jordan." She handed them out without emotion, and Holland took hers though she had no desire to eat it.

"Hey, sis," Brenda said, nudging her red-skirted hip into Holland's.

"Hey." Holland unwrapped her burger and took a bite so she wouldn't have to further the conversation.

"How's Gold Valley?" Apparently Brenda didn't understand the cold vibes Holland was putting off. *And why would she?* Holland wondered. She'd thought it was okay to kiss Jordan while he was still with someone else. And not just someone else. Her very own sister.

The tangled web that seemed so thin and silky in Gold Valley suddenly choked Holland. Her phone buzzed, and she seized onto the opportunity to escape the room. "Excuse me," she managed to say through a closed throat, pushing out the door a moment later.

"Let her go," she heard her mom say amidst Brenda's protest.

Holland didn't care if she was being petty. She was the oldest; she should be more mature; she'd coached herself through all of it before. But a hundred-square-foot hospital room couldn't contain her, and her sister, and Jordan.

"Holland, wait." The masculine voice behind her only made her increase her step. She made it out of the maternity ward, her sandals slapping the tile now as she nearly broke into a run.

"Holland, I'm sorry."

That apology made her freeze. Her chest heaved, and all her carefully placed pieces felt scattered. When she'd found out about Jordan's infidelity with her own sister, Holland had never spoken to him again. She didn't ask him why. Didn't want to know why. She didn't cry or beg or ask for his apology.

The fact that he'd given it to her when she hadn't asked for it hit a nerve deep inside. She turned back to him, her fingers curling into fists. "You're sorry?"

He stood in the hall with his hands stuffed in the pockets of his jeans, one shoulder lifting in a shrug like *I said it once. Not gonna say it again.*

"Did Brenda ask you to apologize?"

"No."

Holland believed him. Her own sister hadn't even apologized for stealing Holland's no-good-for-her boyfriend. *Fiancé*, she reminded herself. She and Jordan had been engaged when Brenda had gotten frisky with him.

In a lot of ways, Holland could thank them for the path she was now on. She was glad she hadn't had to break things off with Jordan only days before their wedding. Hadn't had to explain that she didn't really love him. Hadn't had to tell anyone that she'd made a mistake, that she'd known all along that she'd only started dating Jordan to soothe her pain over her father's death.

She hadn't handled anything well during his quick fight with cancer, hadn't been able to help him after his fall, and her self-loathing and self-blame had taken her down a deep, dark rabbit hole where Jordan had found her.

Holland drew in a deep breath and stared at the face she'd once found so alluring. Dark hair, dark eyes, dark five o'clock shadow though it was barely noon. She'd worked hard to leave the past in the past. Attended church every week to feel the Lord's love for her and seek forgiveness for the mistakes she'd made.

And she believed Jordan could be forgiven too, even if she didn't feel like he deserved it. Even if he hadn't done anything to earn it.

"All right," she said.

He nodded once and ducked back toward the huge plastic door leading back to Lisa's room. "Come on back in," he said. "Brenda won't talk to you again."

For some reason, Holland believed him. She wanted to rid herself of these caged emotions that had been infecting her for the past year, and maybe if she could make it through a meal with Brenda, that healing process could begin.

———

Seven increments of thirty-minutes passed before Jordan said he had to get to work. He and Brenda left, and Holland's mother stepped out into the hall to ask when Lisa could go home. Holland tucked Lisa's hair behind her ear. "Well, that wasn't horrible."

Lisa smiled up at her, but it held gallons of sadness. "Everything about the last couple of days has been horrible."

Holland's heart hurt for her sister. "I know, Lis. I know." She thought of the nephew she'd never seen, and though she'd thought it better for everyone if Lisa gave him to a couple better equipped to take care of a baby, it still hurt.

Some things simply did.

"Some things simply take a lot of time to accept, to understand, to process," she whispered. "You'll get through this."

"Thanks for coming," Lisa said. "I know you didn't want to."

"For you, Lis, I'd go anywhere." And Holland meant what she'd said. She thought about the words she'd sent to Elliott. She was pretty sure she'd meant those too, even if she'd called them an accident.

She pulled out her phone and looked at it. No texts. No missed calls. Had Elliott even looked at his phone? Did he even know what the last three words were that he'd said to her?

"Better go call your cowboy boyfriend," Lisa said.

Holland flinched and dropped her hand to her side. She searched her sister's face. "Mom told you, didn't she?"

"I think it's good you're dating again."

"Can I tell you a secret?"

Lisa's face lit up. "Of course."

"You can't tell Mom."

"My lips are sealed."

"I met him five days ago."

Lisa just blinked at her, and Holland realized that wasn't very scandalous, and certainly not worth keeping secret.

"He kissed me the night we met. We hadn't even gone out."

Now her hazel eyes sparkled. "Wow, Holland. How very unlike you."

"There's something about him." Holland gazed past Lisa, toward the tiny window in the corner of the room. "Do you believe in love at first sight?" She focused back on Lisa, who wore a look halfway between pity and confusion. "It's been…surreal."

"Sounds like it." Lisa shifted in bed. "I'm ready to move on the way you did. Maybe I'll leave Idaho Falls too."

Holland stuffed Elliott into the back of her mind. "Where would you go?"

"Anywhere," Lisa said. "I'm only twenty-four. I can finish my aesthetics training anywhere."

"Do it," Holland said emphatically. "I love Mom, and she'll be sad when you go, but there's something about being on your own, with hardly anyone you know around."

"You have Uncle Wallace and Aunt Wendy."

"I hardly ever see them," she said. "But Cecil has been a real friend." An idea struck her like a bolt of electricity. "Go stay in California with Trudy." Their dad's brother's daughter, Trudy was trying to make it in show business. "She's always looking for a roommate. And you'd have access to a lot of people to practice your makeup and eyelashes on."

"You know, that's not a bad idea," Lisa said, a true smile gracing her face for the first time since Holland had arrived.

"I'm full of good ideas," Holland said, an old joke between the sisters. She always said it when her ideas were definitely bad and usually landed all three of them in a heap of trouble.

Lisa scoffed, the sound quickly morphing into a giggle and then a full-blown laugh. As if the past two years since their father's death hadn't happened, Holland and Lisa dissolved into laughter. All the pain, all the awkwardness, all the heartache was simply gone.

And Holland really needed this moment with her sister. So she held onto it, hoping she'd be able to conjure up the strength she needed to talk to Elliott.

Elliott's phone rang as soon as Nels finished for the day. *Holland.*

He sent it to voicemail, his hour-long ride up the mountain during his lunch break adding time to his day. No one had said anything, but Elliott almost hoped they would so he could confess his I-love-you blunder and figure out what to do about her "accidental" text.

No matter what, he wasn't ready to talk to her yet.

"See you tomorrow," Nels said with a wave, a genuine look of concern on his face. Elliott returned the gesture, smiling as wide as he could, which admittedly wasn't very wide at all.

The door closed behind Nels, and the administration lodge sat in silence. Elliott soaked it up. He normally didn't like spending time with himself, but tonight it felt good. Normally, he didn't like being behind walls, but tonight, they whispered soothing things to him. Normally, he didn't just sit and do nothing, but tonight, the whole earth felt like it was spinning a little slower and he really enjoyed it.

His phone rang again, and this time it was his mother. "Mom?" he asked. "Everything okay? I was just leaving the ranch."

"Just wondering if you'd eaten."

"No, ma'am. Still at work."

"I made that steak and shrimp you like."

Elliott's mouth watered as he thought of the sweet and spicy dish his mother had perfected over the years. "Thanks, Ma."

"Is Holland back yet?"

"Not until tomorrow," he managed to squeeze from his throat. He wanted to see her, talk to her. But for some reason, he didn't want to discuss what they'd said to each other.

"See you soon," his mom said. "Love you, son." She hung up, and Elliott stared at the phone. He believed his mother loved him. His horse. Maybe even his friends. But for some reason, he had never believed a woman could love him. Maybe because no one ever had, and three decades of life had cemented the possibility that he wasn't going to find "the one" for him.

But I have, he thought, remembering that electric spark that had zipped down his spine the first time he laid eyes on Holland. How everything had turned silent and still, until there was only her and him.

He recognized his feelings as fear. It was the same fear he had when Archer had come back to the cabin excited that he'd asked Emery to marry him and she'd said yes. Fear that he'd be left behind once again. Fear that he'd always be alone.

"So don't screw this up," he muttered to himself, pushing out as much of the fear as he could and dialing Holland.

She picked up on the first ring. "Elliott," she said.

"I don't really know if that text was an accident or not," he said, launching right into things. "It doesn't really matter, I guess. I mean, maybe it does. I don't know. What I do know is I've sort of been freaking out for the past four hours, and I wish you were here so I could look into your eyes and know how you really felt."

He took a deep breath, hoping she'd say something and save him from himself. She didn't, so he continued with, "I didn't mean to say 'love you, bye.' It sort of just slipped out. It's what me and my family say to each other, but it was sort of awkward when I said it to you, because it's not like you're my sister or anything."

"I should hope not," Holland said, a playful lilt in her voice that relaxed Elliott.

"And now I'm going to admit something," he said, his panic and fear combining into a terrible storm inside his chest. "I'm scared," was all he could force out.

She gave him a few beats of silence before asking, "Of what?"

"Of this thing between us. It feels huge and all-encompassing, and I met you *five days ago.*" He was near to panting with how much he'd spoken and how intense his blood seemed to be streaming through his veins. "Isn't that a little scary to you?"

"It's a little scary," Holland said, her voice soft and far away. He wanted her right next to him, needed to have her hand in his while they talked.

A noise behind him made him turn, and he saw Jace Lovell standing at the edge of a row of desks, watching him.

"So you come on home," Elliott said. "And we'll go to dinner tomorrow night, and we can talk some more."

"Listen, Elliott, maybe we just need to slow things down a little," she said, a bit of fear in her tone too. "That's easy, right? Take some time to really get to know each other."

Elliott wanted more time with her. A lot more time. So he agreed, and they ended their call.

"Holland?" Jace asked, moving around one of the desks and perching on it.

"Yeah." Elliott nodded several times, his gaze falling to his phone. "We—it's—well, I sort of freaked out today."

"And rode Precious up the mountain. I know."

He got up, hoping he wasn't breaking some sort of girl-friend confidentiality thing. He just needed some help. Someone wiser than him to advise him. "She sent me this text late last night." He tilted the phone so Jace could see it. "She said it was an accident." He looked at the owner of the ranch, who was married with one child and another one on the way.

Jace looked right back at him. "Maybe it was."

"Why would she even type that?"

"Maybe she just wanted to see how it felt to type it." Jace

crossed his arms. "Women aren't like men, Elliott. They think about things we don't think about. Plan their weddings when they're thirteen years old. Holland probably has a fantastical view of how her husband will look on their wedding day, and what kind of dress she'll be wearing, and when you two will tell each other you love each other for the first time."

Elliott could barely keep up with what Jace was saying. "Really?"

Jace smiled in a kind way. "Really. Just ask Belle. We had to wait months to get married so she could have the dress she wanted flown in from New York."

All Elliott could do was blink. "Wow. I had no idea."

"Women aren't like men. Repeat that several times a day." Jace clapped him on the shoulder. "You'll make it past this crisis of faith." He started toward the door. "C'mon now. You've gotta get down to dinner."

Elliott followed Jace out of the building, repeating *women aren't like men* every couple of steps.

———

He pulled up to Holland's house the following evening, his stomach an angry nest of red ants. She'd texted a few times the previous night and again this morning when she got on the road. That was it. Nothing excessive. No more *I love you's*.

She opened the door before he even made it to the steps, and he was rendered weak with the mere sight of her.

Everything he'd felt for her rushed at him, and he couldn't help grinning at her.

"Aren't you a sight for sore eyes?" He climbed the steps and took her in his arms, just like that. Easy. Fun. Light.

Why hadn't he felt like this when she was gone? The fear he'd experienced had evaporated, like it had never existed. He wasn't sure what mind tricks he'd played on himself. What he was sure of was that he liked Holland a whole lot.

He kissed her, a growl starting deep in his throat. She held onto him as she kissed him back, and it was like there were no accidental texts or weird comments said at the end of a phone call.

"This isn't exactly slowing down," she whispered in his ear, sending a cascade of sparks along his skin.

"No, it's not," he said, backing up and rededicating himself to taking things a little slower. "I want to hear all about your sisters, your mom, the trip. Everything." He tucked her hand in his and led her down the steps to his truck.

She started talking, and Elliott listened. "You'll never believe what I saw on the freeway today," she said. "There was this dog strapped to the top of the car." She swiped and tapped on her phone, finally turning it toward him. "Yeah, I took that while I was driving."

He peered at the white, definitely dog-shaped item on top of the SUV. "This can't be real."

"It was a stuffed animal." Holland giggled and looked at her phone. "But it looked so real. For a few seconds, I seriously thought it was a real dog."

He laughed with her and enjoyed the stories she told about her mom and sisters. They made it through ordering and eating by the time she finished. "So things are better?" he asked.

"A little better." She smiled and leaned her face into her hands. "I mean, they're not perfect, but they're better. I don't want to go back to Idaho Falls or anything."

"Of course not." He grinned at her. "You want to walk for a few minutes?"

She nodded and they left his truck at the restaurant in favor of strolling down the street. With October right around the corner, the wind had turned cold, causing Elliott to turn up the collar on his jacket and press his hat firmly onto his head.

"So about us," she said.

"What about us?" He tightened his grip on her shoulder, keeping her close to his side.

"We're okay?"

"I'm great," he said. He was, only because having her here was better than trying to figure out what she meant in a text.

"When I'm ready to say those words to you, Elliott, I'll say them." She stepped in front of him. "Not in a text." She examined his face, looking for something. He wasn't sure what it was, so he didn't know how to give it to her.

"And I won't say it flippantly on the phone," he assured her. "Okay?"

She searched for a moment longer and then nodded. "Okay."

The conversation moved to something else, and Elliott dropped her off an hour later—a passionate kiss against her front door included. Just because they were going slower didn't mean he couldn't kiss her goodnight.

A week passed where he only saw Holland when she came to work with his father. That was comfortable too, and he needed the time to settle into his new job, learn more about her, untangle his own feelings. The snow started the following week, and Elliott only went down to town to check on his father twice.

By Halloween, more snow had fallen than Gold Valley's usual, and no one was leaving the ranch in the evenings. Too slick, or the visibility was too bad, or a winter storm warning had been issued.

So Elliott had retreated to texts. He and Holland could "talk" all night long about his new cabin mate who snored and left his clothes on the bathroom floor.

Gordon Escariot was a tall, ginger-haired cowboy with a loud mouth. Elliott wasn't sure how he'd become the expert on everything from horseshoeing to spring planting to construction, but no matter what they talked about, Gordon knew more than Elliott. Had experienced more. Had an opinion about every little thing, and he never let anything slide.

Having a conversation with him leaves me exhausted, he sent to Holland one night. *I'm coming down tomorrow no matter what. Maybe we can do a late dinner after I visit my parents?*

Sure, she texted. *And ask him about ballet. Think he knows about that?* She included a winking emoji, and Elliott smiled.

But yes, Gordon probably knew all about ballet, including all the French terms. Elliott wasn't willing to find out, and after dinner, he'd taken to his bedroom to avoid talking to the other cowboy. Jace wouldn't be happy about that, but Elliott was in survival mode.

Several cowboys made it down the canyon on a particularly sunny Sunday, and he stepped over to the pew where Holland sat with her cousin. "Hey, beautiful," he drawled.

She looked up at him, a squeal coming from her mouth in the next moment. "Elliott!" She jumped up and flung her arms around him. "You haven't been to church in weeks."

"We're livin' in mud and slush up there, sweetheart." A thrill traveled from the top of his head to the soles of his feet because of her reaction to seeing him. Cecil scooted down to make room for him, and he sat on the end of the row with Holland tucked against his side.

After church, he drove home with her, and Cecil started working in the kitchen. Elliott sat on the couch with Holland curled into him. He closed his eyes and let the peace and slowness of the Sabbath wash over him.

Next thing he knew, Holland was saying his name. "Elliott? Elliott, wake up."

His eyes opened, but he wasn't sure where he was.

"Cecil has lunch ready." Holland's beautiful face filled his vision, and he reached up and cupped her face in his hands. She smiled at him softly, lovingly, and he wondered if she'd look at him like this on their wedding day.

So maybe men did think like women sometimes.

For a few weeks there, he'd wondered if perhaps the

thing that had sparked so hot between them in the beginning was only that—a spark. But he knew gazing at her that there was a whole lot more than a spark to the inferno swirling through his core. He only hoped she could feel it too, and that they'd figure out when to take things to the next level.

CHAPTER 10

"So we're on for Thanksgiving at your parents' house?" Holland asked a few days before Thanksgiving.

"Yeah," Elliott said, his voice hard to hear on the phone line. He hadn't been down from the ranch in two weeks, and Holland was starting to wonder if this winter would ever end. And it hadn't even really started yet. But it had snowed or rained every day for the past thirty days, and she was tired of it. Tired of not having Elliott next to her. Tired of sitting by Cecil at church. Tired of their long-distance relationship, which relied on calls and texts.

"Cecil's coming, right?" he asked. "My mom is gonna love his chocolate tarts."

"It's not traditional Thanksgiving cuisine," Holland said, flipping another page in her magazine. Even Cecil had had to work late tonight. "He's worried about that. He said he can do pecan pie. Or pumpkin, though he said he needs to find a new recipe because he doesn't like the one he's been using."

Holland didn't get the difference between recipes if they both made the same thing, but she'd humored Cecil and said that yeah, definitely, he needed to find a better pumpkin pie recipe.

"He can bring whatever he wants. Or nothing. My mom doesn't care."

"All right." Holland looked at the lip color on the model in the magazine, wondering if it would be too bright for a wedding. She circled it anyway, deciding to do a lip color challenge for the month of December. Ask her patients which one they liked best for a spring bride.

Or summer, she told herself, as things between her and Elliott had slowed to a crawl. It was really hard to kiss the man when he rarely left the ranch. Still, whenever he did come into town, she had to compete for his attention with his parents, and now with Cecil's cooking.

He did kiss her completely every time they were together, and she had pinned so many wedding dresses to her board, perhaps she should be thinking of a fall wedding instead. After all, it would take her a couple of weeks just to go through the pins and narrow down her choices based on season, color, and price. Even then, she'd be lucky to be able to choose a favorite.

Their conversation ended, and Holland divided up the increments she needed to endure until she'd see him at his mother's house for Thanksgiving dinner. Over one hundred and fifty. She sighed, abandoned her magazine, and pulled out her phone to text Lisa.

Over the past couple of months since Lisa had had the baby, she seemed to be doing better and better every time Holland talked to her. She smiled at Lisa's, *I have some good news!*

Gratitude descended on her, and she was glad she had something to fill the time this winter evening as snow fell outside her window.

Thanksgiving morning dawned with the scent of chocolate, and Holland took a few extra minutes in bed to smile to herself. She found Cecil in the kitchen, up to his elbows in chocolate pudding.

"Help me put plastic wrap on these," he said. "So they don't get a skin." He seemed a little frazzled, so Holland jumped in and helped with the plastic wrap. Cecil carried the trays of covered tarts into the garage. "It's cool enough in there to act like a refrigerator." He clapped his hands together when he returned to the kitchen. "So, are we excited for this Thanksgiving dinner?"

"Sure," Holland said, pulling out a coffee mug and a carton of cream. "Are you?"

"I'm glad I don't have to go to my parents' house," he said. "Jules and *Gregory* will be there. All happily married with children and dogs and blah."

Holland poured herself a cup of coffee and contemplated her cousin's words. "You're still a valuable member of your family," she said. "Just because you're divorced doesn't make you inferior."

"I know it doesn't. I just feel like I don't belong."

Holland quirked her eyebrow at him. "And you want to come hang out with me and my boyfriend at his parents' house? How is that better?"

Cecil bobbed his head, which meant he had a secret, and Holland's curiosity burst through the roof. "Cecil," she said, drawing his name out. "Why do you want to come to Elliott's house so badly?" She glanced around. It was barely eight AM, and the tarts were already done. He must've gotten up at five to get the shells baked and cooled enough to pour in the pudding.

He sighed and leaned into the counter. "Merry said her god-daughter would be there. She thinks we'll be… compatible."

Holland stared at him, his words taking a few moments to organize themselves into meaning. "You're meeting a woman today?"

"For the first time," Cecil said. "Though I've texted her a few times. So I would appreciate it if you'd be all…." He waved his hand around like he was completing a magic spell. "Complimentary of me. My cooking. All that."

Holland grinned. "Of course I'll be complimentary. You're a great guy, Cecil." She sipped her coffee. "Sorry it didn't work out with Lena."

"Elliott was right. There was no spark." He shrugged. "Maybe there will be today."

"Maybe." Holland put her coffee on the counter and stood. "I'm going to shower. Lunch isn't until one."

"But Merry said to come anytime," he called after her.

"No earlier than ten," she said over her shoulder. "Elliott's planning to be there at ten." And while Holland liked his parents just fine, she didn't want to hang out over there without Elliott.

She and Cecil arrived at the Hawthorne's closer to eleven, mostly because Cecil didn't want to be seen as "overeager." By the time they stepped out of the howling wind and gray skies, Holland was a bit on the overeager side. She hadn't seen Elliott in over a week, and she didn't know she could miss a person so much.

He stood in the kitchen, saying something to his mother, who manned several pots on the stove. Another woman rose from the couch, where Sean also sat, her blue eyes only for Cecil.

"You must be Tara," he said, extending his hand for her to shake.

"And you must be Cecil." She smiled and put her hand in his. Holland watched their exchange carefully, noting how sparkly Tara's eyes were and how wide Cecil's smile.

"Hey, beautiful." Elliott joined her and slipped his hand along her waist. She promptly forgot about Cecil and his new lady friend. Only the sight of Elliott's happy-hazel eyes existed. The scent of his woodsy cologne. The warmth and roughness of his touch.

"Elliott." Her gaze dropped to his mouth, and he smiled

as he gently nudged her toward the living room. Toward privacy.

"Excuse us," he said, glancing around to everyone as he took her hand and led her out into the garage. A chill skated across her skin, only partially because of the temperature outside. But mostly because Elliott swiped off his cowboy hat and gazed down at her with love and desire riding in his expression.

"I missed you," he said, dipping his head as if he'd taste her mouth. He didn't, which shot disappointment through her. But he trailed his lips along her jaw and nipped at her earlobe, and everything was just fine.

"I don't like it when you're sequestered up at the ranch," she whispered, slipping her fingers into his hair.

He ran his hands up her sides and cupped her face in his palms. "I can see that." He grinned as if he'd just won the lottery, and she tipped up on her toes to kiss him. She poured everything she had into the kiss, and he responded eagerly. Maybe overeagerly. Holland didn't care. She craved his touch, his kiss, his presence.

"Holland," he said breathlessly, stroking his thumb across her bottom lip before he kissed her again. Deeper and deeper she fell in love with him, sure that his absence had made her heart grow fonder for him.

"Holland," he said again, pulling back completely this time. "Holland."

"What?" she asked, searching his face for any hint of what he wanted to say.

"I love you," he said, a smile bursting onto his face. "I've known it since the moment I laid eyes on you right in there." He half-nodded behind him, indicating the house. "I'm so grateful for you in my life." He tracked his fingers down the side of her face.

A party started in Holland's chest, little bursts and pops of excitement mingled with disbelief. "I'm in love with you too," she whispered.

He chuckled, shook his head the slightest bit, and kissed her again.

————

Holland started living her life in days, not half-hours. Five days of work. One day of church. One day off, and not always a Saturday. Seventeen days of bad weather.

Elliott's schedule was easier, but getting down into town wasn't. Holland stopped by his parents' house though his father's physical therapy had ended a while ago. She made sure their sidewalks got shoveled and they had the groceries they needed. All the stuff Elliott would normally do, if he was able to get down the canyon.

Christmas came and went, and still Elliott didn't propose. He gave great gifts, sure. Just not any that came in black ring boxes and sparkled like the stars.

One of her New Year's resolutions was to bring up marriage with him. They'd talked about everything else—children, jobs, hopes, dreams, all of it. But he had not once mentioned a wedding.

She'd started weeding through the dresses she'd pinned,

and eliminating colors, and she may have even stopped into the jewelry store downtown to see what the selection was like.

The first week of January, Holland got a text from Lisa that said *I made it!* along with a picture of her with her feet in the ocean, her skirt gathered around her knees in one hand, her face an absolute picture of joy.

She had made arrangements to go to California, and Holland's heart expanded with happiness for her sister. Even if she was a bit jealous of the golden sunshine in the picture while she had to deal with yet another winter storm warning.

So glad! she sent back. *Send lots of pictures. It's currently forty below zero in Montana.* Yet somehow her car started every morning and she managed to make it to her patient's homes though the roads were slick and snow-packed.

A few days after Lisa had arrived in California, the sun broke through the clouds in Gold Valley. Holland immediately texted Elliott and asked if he could come down for dinner. He agreed, and Holland hurried through her appointments and headed back to Cecil's.

She took precious time to curl her hair, apply eye make-up, and slip into a tight pair of jeans and a sweater the color of blueberries.

Knocking sounded on the door, and her excitement soared toward the sky. She took a few extra seconds to slip into her ankle boots, which added a couple of inches to her height, before pulling open the door with a smile and a giggle already emanating from her mouth.

But Elliott didn't stand there.

The light laugh died in her throat.

"Hey, sis." Brenda cocked her hip, the white fur along her neck shifting slightly.

Holland couldn't respond, almost like the sight of her sister had muted her vocal chords. Her thoughts, however, raced around a track screaming *What in the world is Brenda doing here?*

"Can I come in?" her sister asked. "It's freezing out here."

CHAPTER 11

Elliott gripped the steering wheel as he rounded the last bend and the horseshoe shaped waterfalls came into view. For a few minutes there, he'd kept a prayer streaming from his mouth, begging the Lord to get him down to the valley safely.

He had no idea how he was going to navigate that road again tonight. He had a distinct feeling he shouldn't, but he wasn't looking forward to sleeping in his clothes either. He hadn't been planning on seeing his parents at all tonight, and unless he called them, he'd have to cut short his dinner date with Holland to be sure he arrived before they locked up for the night.

After he pulled up to the curb at Holland's house, he called his mom. "Hey, Ma," he said. "I came down to see Holland tonight, and I don't think I can get back up to the ranch safely. Will you leave the door open for me? I'll lock up when I get there."

She agreed, and Elliott faced Holland's place. He'd checked to see how late the jewelry store stayed open, and if they went there first, maybe their dinner would go later than even Elliott knew.

Nerves assaulted him, but he steadied himself. He loved Holland. She loved him. The next step involved diamonds and churches and a place where they could sleep in each other's arms.

Another car sat in the driveway, but it was probably Tara's. Holland had reported that Cecil and Tara had hit it off at Thanksgiving and a relationship had started soon after that. No matter what, he couldn't just blurt out his idea of going to the jewelry store before dinner.

He cursed his choice of slippery footwear but made it to the front porch without incident. He knocked and waited where he usually just went in. He didn't want to interrupt Cecil and Tara, though, so he shoved his hands in his pockets and tried to breathe shallowly so his lungs wouldn't freeze together.

The door opened to reveal a shapely woman who wasn't Tara or Holland. She wore a dress that seemed sewn into her skin and didn't provide nearly the warmth she needed for a winter night like tonight.

Her hair fell over her bare shoulders in curls, and her ruby red lips parted into a smile. "Hello there, handsome," she purred.

Elliott glanced to his right to check the house number. Surely he'd gotten it wrong. Nope. This was the right house. "Oh, uh, I'm looking—"

"Elliott." Holland's relieved voice sank right into his soul. She hurried up behind the other woman, and he saw some similarities in them. "Back up, Brenda, and let him in."

Brenda.

The name rang in Elliott's head. Holland hadn't mentioned her sister stopping by for a visit, and he tried to make eye contact with her. She wouldn't look fully at him though, not for longer than a heartbeat. She tripped over the rug and mumbled something to herself.

Elliott had never seen her so anxious, and he immediately despised her sister for causing it.

"Did you bring them?" she asked, finally meeting his eye.

"Bring…? Oh, yeah." He started nodding when he realized she was playing a game here. He had no idea what the rules were, or what to say next.

"Did you leave them in your truck?" Holland tucked her already flat hair, a gesture that normally he found cute, adorable.

Brenda circled him like he was live bait, and his skin crawled. "Yeah. Yes," he said. "Should we go check them out?"

"Oh, let her go," Brenda said lazily, like Holland would do whatever she said. "It's cold out there." She brushed her body against his, causing him to flinch away from her. She and Holland were so different, and Elliott could hardly believe they were sisters.

"I'll go with you," he said, making a hasty escape toward the front door. Holland didn't even put on a coat before following him out.

"She just showed up five minutes ago," she said, her breath hanging in the air in front of her. "I can't get rid of her. She said she and Jordan broke up, and she didn't have anywhere else to go, and Cecil's out with Tara, and I didn't know—" She sucked in a breath, her face lit with panic.

Elliott put his hands on her shoulders and slid his fingers down her arm. Back up. "It's okay," he said. "Let's just go."

She nodded, and he helped her into his truck and got the heater going. Holland stayed way over on her side, and Elliott missed her presence right beside him.

"So what sounds good tonight?" he asked, hoping to break her out of the funk she'd obviously fallen into. With disappointment and defeat, he told himself there would be no diamond-ring-shopping tonight.

She didn't answer. He drove toward downtown, thinking they could just grab something and go eat it at his parents' house. Or in the truck. She didn't seem like she wanted to be around people.

Or maybe she just didn't want to be around Brenda.

Elliott wasn't sure, because he'd never seen Holland act like this before.

"Holland?" he asked once he'd made it downtown. "Burritos? Hamburger? We can drive over to the falls and eat." It was already too dark to see much, but she'd never minded that before. Of course, they'd eaten and then kissed until his mouth felt bruised before. No light necessary for that.

She turned toward him, her dark eyes wide and worried. "I think we should…you should go back to the ranch."

"I'm not goin' back to the ranch tonight," he said with a frown. "I almost died coming down that canyon." He peered at her. "What's going on?"

"I don't want Brenda to know you're my boyfriend," she said in a rush of air and words. "If she knows, she'll try to steal you from me."

Elliott thought she was interested whether she knew he was Holland's boyfriend or not, but he kept that thought to himself. "She has no chance, sweetheart." He made his voice as gentle as possible. "I'm in love with you." He added a smile to the statement.

Holland rolled her eyes and flipped her hair. "Yeah, I've heard that before." She cinched her arms across her chest, and Elliott's pulse pinched.

"So you want me to take you back there?" Confusion dripped from every word.

"Yes," she said. "I can tell her we had to run back to your place for something real quick. No big deal."

"Holland, I don't get it. She doesn't know we're dating? You didn't tell your family?" She'd told him she'd mentioned him to her family. If she hadn't….

She looked at him with real fear in her expression. "I told my mom and Lisa. Swore them to secrecy." Her gaze wandered to his hat and back to his eyes. "Please, Elliott."

He didn't see what choice he had. "All right." He returned her to her house, where Brenda's face peeped through the window. He wouldn't even get to kiss her. Sure enough, Holland leapt from the truck almost before it had even come to a full stop. She didn't look back as she hurried up the walkway and went back in the house.

Elliott had no idea what had just happened. What he did know was there was now a giant Holland-shaped hole in his life.

———

He'd stopped living in thirty-minute increments months ago. But now, without any communication with Holland, every minute felt endless. He went back to coaching himself to make it through the next half-hour. Then the next one.

Life on the ranch during a brutal winter like this one wasn't fun. Twenty-five men all cooped up together most of the time. Mud and muck everywhere. And to top it off, Elliott's cabin mate had alienated most of the other cowboys, and some of them had started avoiding Elliott as well.

He sat behind the desk and managed the minimal chores needed to keep the animals alive and the ranch operational. Jace had the cowboys cleaning every available surface in every building on the ranch, but that work had run out already.

"Another movie day?" Archer asked when he walked in.

"It's that or risk frostbite," Elliott muttered. At this point, the frostbite would be better than staring at his silent phone and willing Holland to send him even one word.

Hey.

Hello.

She's gone.

How are you?

Can you come down?

So he wanted more than one word from her. He wanted a whole lot more than one word.

Archer didn't join the other cowboys loading up with popcorn and sodas from the kitchen. He pulled the nearest chair over and sat down. "What's eating you?"

Elliott didn't see any point in keeping it a secret. "Holland."

"I thought you guys were great," Archer said, twisting the wedding band on his left ring finger. "Last time we talked, you were going to propose just as soon as you could get down the canyon."

Elliott started nodding, his brain knocking around inside his head. "Her sister came to town."

"So?"

"So…she's freaked out. She hasn't answered any of my calls in days. She won't text me back. I think she may have actually blocked my number."

Archer frowned and squinted at him. "Why would she do that?"

"There's some bad blood between her and Brenda."

"Brenda Marsh?" Archer said the name with too much interest to be casual.

Elliott glanced up from his dark phone screen. "Yeah. You know her?"

His best friend cleared his throat. "No, I don't *know* her. I know *of* her."

"She's been in town for four days."

"And she moves fast, apparently."

"What does that mean?"

"It means she's got herself a boyfriend—or two—already."

Elliott didn't know what to think of that. He wondered how Holland was weathering all of this, and he really needed to talk to her. The urge to call her hit him right in the throat, making it impossible to swallow.

"Do you think I'd be missed today?" he asked, glancing over his shoulder to the wall where the movie played.

"Not even a little," Archer said. "Jace has the chores on rotation. We'll be fine." He stood and stretched. "Where are you goin'?"

"I've got to go see Holland."

Archer nodded, and Elliott headed out to get his keys. The canyon wasn't too terrible, and he made it to the valley in one piece, no prayers needed. Holland worked in patient's homes, so he had no idea where to find her. With her on radio silence, his only other choice was her cousin.

He found Cecil in the produce department at the supermarket, a cheerful smile on his face. At least until he saw Elliott.

"Hey," Cecil said, continuing to mound avocadoes. "I know why you're here."

"How is she? She won't talk to me. I don't even know what I did."

"It's not you." Cecil sighed. "She's trying to protect you."

"From Brenda."

Cecil nodded. "That woman is…not nice."

"You're letting her stay with you?"

"I told her she could stay for a week."

Three more days. Could Elliott survive for three more days without Holland in his life? He wasn't sure why he was reacting this way. He'd spent weeks sequestered up at the ranch—but he'd had Holland only a text away.

This new distance between them felt too wide, too deep, to cross.

He sighed and glanced around like the apples and oranges would be able to help him. "So I just—what? Go back up to the ranch and wait for Brenda to leave town?"

Cecil shrugged. "That's one way to do it."

Elliott didn't like that option. He wanted the world to know he was Holland's and she was his. Even her sister. *Especially* her sister.

"Will she be home tonight?" Elliott asked.

"I don't have her schedule memorized," Cecil said with a wry smile. "But yes, I believe her night patients were last night."

Elliott nodded and turned toward the exit. "Thanks, Cecil."

"Might want to lose the cowboy hat," he called after Elliott.

Elliott twisted back to the other man. "Why?"

"I've heard Brenda say she really likes a man in a cowboy hat. Could throw her off your scent."

"Thanks." Elliott pushed his hat further on his head. He didn't want to make himself unattractive to Brenda. He wanted to show her that he, cowboy hat and all, was in love with her sister, and that Brenda had absolutely no chance of changing that.

CHAPTER 12

Holland groaned as she massaged her neck, rotating it to the left and then the right. It had been an incredibly difficult four days, and she couldn't wait until Brenda left. Cecil had graciously said she could stay for a week, but it felt like she'd been in town for a year already.

As long as she doesn't find out about Elliott, Holland told herself for the umpteenth time. She kept her phone on silent all the time and constantly erased his text messages without responding to them. Hopefully he would understand. In three days, she'd make him understand.

When she pulled up to the house, both Cecil's and Brenda's cars were already there. His *Hurry home for dinner* text made so much more sense now. Holland wondered if her sister knew that she made everyone around her uncomfortable.

Probably. She probably did it on purpose.

Holland knew she didn't do anything without careful thought, and she really wanted to know what Brenda was doing in Gold Valley. She'd never shown interest in coming to Montana previously. She'd even sneered at Holland once she'd found out Holland had come to Gold Valley to start fresh, like the town itself was beneath her.

She pushed into the house and said, "Hey, Cecil."

The relief on his face would've been comical if it wasn't Brenda causing all the turmoil. She glanced over from her seated position at the bar, and Holland looked away as she dropped her keys into her purse.

Then Elliott rose from the couch, only steps from her. "Hey, beautiful," he said, very clearly and definitely loud enough for Brenda to hear.

"What are you doing here?" she asked, her heart thumping like wild horse's hooves. She glanced at Cecil, who wore a halfway sympathetic expression on his face. He'd told her not to hide Elliott from Brenda, but Holland didn't trust—

She cut off the thought, because it was too painful to let it continue to completion. She wasn't sure if she didn't trust herself or she didn't trust Elliott, but neither prospect brought much comfort.

"I miss you," he said much quieter. He came around the couch and gathered her into his arms. She went because he was Elliott Hawthorne and she loved him. But she stiffened after only two breaths of his wonderful cologne.

"So he spoke the truth." Brenda's words dripped with poisoned honey. "He said he was your boyfriend, but I didn't really believe him." She tiptoed two blood-red finger-nails up the zipper on Elliott's jacket.

"Why wouldn't you believe me?" he asked.

"She just…doesn't seem your type." She sized up Holland and definitely found her lacking for the handsome cowboy.

"She's my type." He put an arm protectively around her, but Holland wished he wasn't here at all. Didn't he understand that Brenda *liked* a challenge? Thrived on it?

"Dinner's ready," Cecil announced, and Brenda turned back to the kitchen.

"I want to support you in this." Elliott's heated breath touched her neck as he whispered in her ear. "Don't make me go, okay?" He stepped away and clapped his hands, proclaiming, "You are the best cook in town, Cecil."

Brenda rolled her eyes and zeroed in on Holland, a clear message in her expression. *You lied to me. Said you weren't dating anyone.*

Which Holland had done. She'd been praying to know how to get rid of Brenda for days, what to say to her, all of it. God hadn't been extremely forthcoming, and Holland hoped everything wasn't about to blow up.

"So how serious are you two?" she asked as soon as grace was finished.

"Serious," Elliott said while Holland couldn't seem to formulate an answer of any kind. It seemed impossible that he wasn't afraid of Brenda, but he sure didn't seem to be.

Holland's hand froze with a piece of chicken picatta halfway to her mouth. Why was *she* afraid of Brenda? Why had she given her that power? The power to duck into closets in the hospital. The power to leave her sister's bedside during a difficult emotional time. The power to hide her own boyfriend.

"Hopefully diamond serious," Holland said, giving Elliott a meaningful look.

His cheeks colored and he focused on his food. "Oh, that's comin'."

"When?" Brenda asked, practically salivating at all this juicy gossip. She hadn't even touched her food.

It just so happened that Holland would like to know when too, so she just cut another bite and watched Elliott.

"You know, Cecil, I think coming over here tonight *was* a bad idea." He grinned good-naturedly though, and his gaze caught hers for a brief moment before he glanced down. "So, Brenda, why are you in town?" he asked, deftly changing the subject without providing an answer about the diamond.

She pouted, which usually turned men to putty in her hands. Holland had a hard time keeping her expression neutral.

"My boyfriend broke up with me," she said, the hint of emotion in her voice. "I just couldn't stay in town."

"Too bad," Elliott said, making it sound like he really thought so. "Where are you headed?"

"I might just stay here," she said.

"No," Holland said at the same time Cecil blurted, "No, Brenda. One week, remember?" At least her cousin was solidly on Holland's side. She'd texted both Lisa and her mother to find out what Brenda wanted in Gold Valley. If Holland could give her what she wanted, she'd leave.

But neither of them had known. Lisa had left for California before the break-up, and her mom hadn't even known Brenda wasn't in Idaho Falls anymore. It had only taken a few texts and a few minutes to confirm that she and Jordan had indeed broken up.

"I'll get my own place, Cecil," Brenda said acidly. "Calm down."

"You're not staying here," Holland said.

"You don't own Gold Valley." Brenda trilled out a laugh.

Holland put down her fork and leaned forward. "Yes, I do, Brenda. I came here to start my life again after *you* ruined it. This *is* my town, and you are *not* staying here."

She'd never stood up to her younger sister this way, and the way Brenda's eyes narrowed proved it. Vaguely, she felt Elliott's hand cover hers, heard him say something in his beautiful bass voice. But she didn't look away from her sister. In this battle over Gold Valley, she was going to win.

The next thing she knew, Elliott was towing her down the hall and into her bedroom. "What?" she tried, but he put his forefinger on her lips.

"Just listen to me," he said in a barely audible voice. "Please, Holland. Just listen for a second."

She nodded, stunned into silence by the urgency in his eyes.

"You're giving her exactly what she wants," he said. "A fight. Who cares if she lives here?"

"*I* care," Holland said. Emotions—all the negative ones

she'd stuffed into the back of her soul when she'd left Idaho Falls—came rushing forward. "You don't understand what she's like. I just can't have her living here. I can't stand the thought of running into her at the grocery store, or seeing her when we're getting waffles." She swiped at the tears streaming down her face. "I can't, Elliott."

"Sweetheart." He gathered her into his chest, right where she fit and always wanted to be. "You're not seein' the whole picture. Sometimes we can't see around the bend. But then we get to that part of the road, and everything makes sense."

"I don't understand." She held onto him tightly, trying to draw strength from him.

"You know why she's here, right?" he asked.

"No." The helplessness in Holland felt all-encompassing, close to drowning her.

"She wants to see if you managed to find happiness after what she did to you." He stepped back and gazed at her with those gorgeous eyes. He held her by her shoulders. "So show her that you did. With me. That we're happy together."

"She'll steal you from me."

He smiled a soft smile and shook his head. "Not gonna happen. She's desperate to know she can find happiness again. And, I think…I think she wants to make things right between the two of you. She knows she can't be happy until she does."

Holland didn't want to give her that satisfaction. At the same time, she desperately wanted to let go of the lead balloons that had been weighing her down for so long.

"Holland." Elliott tipped her chin up, forcing her to look

at him. "I love you." He kissed her, slow and soft and sweet. She could lose herself to him—she already had. She broke the connection between them sooner than she would've liked, overcome with love for him.

"Thank you," she breathed, starting to feel more like herself than she had since Brenda had shown up on the front doorstep.

"C'mon," he said. "Let's go show her what happiness looks like." He slung his arm over her shoulder and went with her back down the hall.

Holland straightened and didn't allow herself to wither under Brenda's scrutiny. "Brenda," she said calmly. "This is Elliott Hawthorne. He's my boyfriend."

His fingers tightened on her upper arm, and his lips skated across her temple. "Now that we have that all established, let's see what Cecil made for dessert."

"Donut holes." He pushed away from the table and practically ran into the kitchen. Elliott followed, leaving Brenda and Holland alone on the other side of the counter. Holland stared at her sister, angry at herself for letting her sister dictate her life for the past year.

She turned away and moved into the living room. Brenda followed with the question, "How long have you been dating him?"

"Four or five months," Holland said.

"And you love him?"

Holland sighed, the twitch of a smile playing with her mouth. "It was love at first sight." She crossed her legs and watched Brenda sink into the armchair across from her. "What happened with you and Jordan?"

She waggled her fingers. "Oh, you know."

"No, I don't know."

Brenda sobered and met Holland's eye. "He was guilt-ridden over what we'd done to you. Happy now?"

"A little, yeah," Holland said. "Did he cheat on you?"

"Not that I'm aware of."

"Then I still had it worse." She flashed a tight non-smile at her sister, searching for the forgiveness that would help her get around this bend in the road. "But I'm sorry if you're upset over the break-up."

Brenda nodded and tucked a clump of curls behind her ear. "Holland, I—" She cleared her throat. "I'm sorry about what we did to you, too. I shouldn't have—it was wrong of me to be with him when he was still with you."

The apology sounded like a gong in Holland's ears, and she suddenly realized it didn't matter if Brenda was being sincere or not. Didn't matter if she was sorry or not.

She could forgive her anyway.

"It's forgiven," she whispered. "Let's forget about it."

A weight seemed to lift from Brenda's face at the same rate it floated off Holland's shoulders.

Elliott and Cecil joined them, one carrying a platter of donut holes and the other flourishing chocolate sauce.

Holland gazed up at her boyfriend, finally able to see around the bend and toward a future with him.

CHAPTER 13

"So this is Precious." Elliott patted the bay horse's cheeks as Holland reached to stroke her nose.

"Will we keep her at our house or up here?" she asked.

"Probably up here," he said. "I'll still come up every day to work and all that."

"And you still need to ask me to marry you," she said.

He grinned and nodded, this playful banter between them common now that her sister had left town. "It's—"

"Coming, I know." Holland nudged him with her shoulder. "You better have one amazing proposal, buddy."

"I don't," he said. "Maybe I just want it to be a surprise. Maybe you should go one day without reminding me we're not engaged."

She tipped her head back and laughed. He swept her into his arms and kissed her. "I was just teasing," he said roughly. "Remind me everyday, okay?" He covered her mouth with his again, deepening their kiss as he breathed in the fresh sunshine scent of her.

He liked kissing her in the stable, pressed up against the door like this. Of course, he liked kissing her in his truck too. On her front porch. Everywhere he could.

He'd learned that he couldn't marry her and live on the ranch. Archer and Emery lived right at the base of the canyon, and he'd started looking for housing in that area too. Jace had promised him a housing allowance, which meant Elliott still had enough money saved to buy Holland a ring.

And Valentine's Day was coming right up. What better night to propose than February fourteenth?

"Hey, comin' through."

Elliott pulled away from Holland, who ducked behind his shoulder as Archer joined them in the stables. "Hey, Arch," he said, a fair bit of embarrassment at being caught making out with his girlfriend.

"Elliott." He ducked his head. "Holland. Boss is two minutes behind me." He grinned as he opened the stall for the horse he'd been working with. "Best not let him see you two kissin' in here like that."

Elliott chuckled, half from embarrassment and half from nerves. Holland's whole face was bright red, which only made Elliott want to kiss her again. Instead, he took her back outside to the chilly January weather. "So I'll come down for dinner tonight," he said.

"All right," she drawled in her sexy, fake cowgirl accent. "I want diamonds." Her hand flew to her mouth. "Oops. Did

I say diamonds? I meant *drumsticks*. And wings. Mm. *Buffalo* wings."

She backed away from him, a playful smile on her face, until their fingers separated. He watched her go, wondering if he could wait two more weeks to propose.

"You better put a ring on that woman's finger soon," Jace said, approaching with a horse. "I can't believe she's stuck around this long."

"Aw, come on, boss," Archer said. "Elliott's really handsome."

"Shut up," he told them as they started to laugh. "She said I better have a really good proposal."

"Yeah, you better," Jace agreed.

He turned to his friends with panic streaming through him. "I've got nothing." He volleyed his gaze between them. "Help me."

"I'm bad at that kind of stuff," Jace said, continuing toward the stable.

"Me too," Archer said.

"You stood on a roof in a Santa suit," Elliott said. "That was amazing."

"*That* wasn't the proposal." Archer clapped him on the shoulder. "You'll think of something."

But *something* never came, and Elliott started down the canyon with bees in his chest. Up to the door with hesitation in his step. He knocked and entered the house without waiting for someone to let him in.

And he caught Cecil and Tara in an embrace much like

the one he'd been sharing with Holland in the stables earlier that day.

"Oh, wow, sorry." Elliott backed out of the house, bringing the door closed in front of him, his nerves now firing like cannons. Why hadn't he waited to enter? He turned back to the driveway, and he didn't see Tara's car. That was why.

The temperature had to be way below freezing, but his face felt so hot he didn't notice.

"Psst."

He turned toward the sound and found Holland leaning in the garage. She waved at him, a smile already on her face, and he moved toward her. "I just walked in on Cecil and Tara," he whispered. "I didn't see her car."

"It's in the shop," Holland said. "Cecil picked her up on his way home from work."

"I feel like a fool." Elliott slipped his arms around Holland. "Was it their first kiss?"

"I don't think so." She burrowed into his chest, wrapping her arms around his back. "I'm glad they're getting along so well. Cecil's been so happy since Thanksgiving."

"Hm." Elliott swayed on his feet, his mind wandering to what it would be like to hold her this way, her in a white, lacy dress, him in a tuxedo....

"Come on," he said. "I'm starving."

She sat right next to him in the truck as they drove downtown, chatting about a new patient she'd started working with. She fell silent when he didn't go all the way into the restaurant-heavy section of town.

"Where are we going?" she asked, peering out the windshield.

Elliott wanted to prolong the moment, keep her on the edge of her seat, buy himself some more time to come up with a romantic proposal.

He had nothing.

He pulled to the side of the road and took a deep breath. "I was going to plan this big elaborate proposal for Valentine's Day," he said. "But I don't want to wait anymore. I want the whole world to know you're mine and I'm yours."

A smile touched her eyes and her chin started to wobble a little.

"I've said this before, Holland, but I really did fall in love with you that night in my parents' living room. I can still remember how everything fell into complete silence. I could only see you, and I wanted to know who you were and how to get you into my life." He ducked his head, the memories from that night so loud and vibrant in his mind.

"I love you, Holland Marsh. Will you marry me?"

A single tear slithered out of the corner of her eye. "Yes."

"I don't have a ring," he said. "That's why we're here. I've seen your pinboard, and I thought you'd like to pick out your own diamond."

Her eyes shone with tears, with hope, with love. "You've seen my pinboard?"

Elliott wished he could recall the words. "Well, yeah. I saw you looking at it one day at church. I can search the Internet, I'll have you know."

"I didn't even know the ranch had WiFi." She giggled, and he laughed with her.

"Well, we do." He rubbed the tip of his nose against hers. "And I have a desk job now. So. Which dress are you going to go with?"

She practically melted into him. "I have absolutely no idea."

He gestured down the street a bit, where the bright white lights of the jewelry store beamed into the darkness. "Well, let's go get your diamond."

He started to get out, but she put her hand on his arm. "Elliott," she said.

"Hm?"

"I love you, cowboy."

And he believed her, a keen sense of warmth flowing through him. He leaned closer and kissed her, this time just as magical and magnificent as the first time.

––––––

Read on for a sneak peek at **HER RESTLESS COWBOY,** the first full-length book in the Steeple Ridge Romance series, which focuses on 4 brothers and their journeys toward happily-ever-after.

Ben Buttars thundered down the stairs, a bit of dust rising into the air from his boots. Or maybe that was from the wooden stairs that hadn't been swept in a while. The boss hired a maid service that came in twice a month, but once spring thawed and all the mud dried to dirt, not even a daily cleaning could keep the two-story house dust-free.

"Something smells good," his oldest brother, Sam, said as he pushed through the back door and into the kitchen, where Ben had just entered. He snatched a pair of oven mitts from the counter and opened the door to a blast of heat.

Ben flinched away lest he get burned. "Soft pretzels. Your afternoon snack." He grinned, though the memory of his mother always came with the sight and smell of the last snack she'd made for him before she died. Ben had perfected her recipe over the past ten years.

"Mustard?" Sam bent to look in the fridge.

"Already on the counter. Ketchup too." Ben slid the sheet tray onto the stovetop and gazed down at the perfectly browned snack.

"No one eats ketchup on pretzels," Sam said.

"I do." Ben tossed him a grin just as both of their phones sounded. He groaned while Sam simply checked his without any alarm on his face. But Ben was supposed to have the afternoon off before meeting with the recreational director about…something his boss had seemed deliberately dodgy about. And he'd been planning to stuff himself silly with salty pretzels and ketchup.

"Horses out above pasture six," Sam said, lifting his eyes to Ben's. Out of his three brothers, Ben looked the most like Sam—the most like their father, who'd had eyes the color of russet potato skins and hair several shades darker than that. The twins, who sat in between Ben and Sam, had lighter hair and their mother's darker eyes. All four boys had freckles and broad shoulders and a love for the outdoors.

Only Ben had been a minor when their parents had passed away. Only Ben had been forced to leave high school before he'd graduated. Only Ben hadn't dated someone in the last decade.

"Right now?" he asked, and he hated that it sounded more like a whine than a question.

"Right now." Sam started toward the back door, smashing his cowboy hat lower onto his head.

"But the pretzels—"

"They'll keep." Sam's voice filtered back toward him just

before the screen door slammed. Frustration threaded through Ben. "They'll keep" was Sam's standard answer for everything.

What should we do with Mom and Dad's stuff?

It'll keep.

Shouldn't we go back to Wyoming? Sell the house?

It'll keep.

Ben cast one last look at the steaming pretzels—which would be ten times better hot—before following his brother out of the house they shared. The blue May sky of Vermont stretched before him, the barns and public parking areas of Steeple Ridge Farm just steps from the house.

The pastures, however, lay to the north and west, in the same direction of the wooded area where Ben liked to let his horse wander after a long day of farm work. He strode toward the back barn, where they housed the farm's horses, including his mare, Willow.

Her dark brown coat glistened, because Ben took immaculate care of her. He'd allow dust in the house, but certainly not on his horse. "All right, girl," he said as he put the saddle on and cinched it. "Let's do this quickly, okay? Because I made pretzels." He led the horse out of the barn and swung onto her back.

Steeple Ridge boarded horses, and the five they had from a barn in northern New York had been nothing but trouble since they'd arrived last week. They seemed to have a knack for finding—or creating—weaknesses in fences and running wild through the woods until they came to the stream.

Bracken ferns grew there, and these New York horses seemed to have developed a taste for it, though if they ate enough of it they could experience a loss of nerve function. As the manager of the boarding stable, Sam didn't much want to return nerve-damaged horses to the New York clients. With hot pretzels still on his mind, saving the horses from their own fern obsession was a toss-up for Ben.

He joined his brothers and they spread out into the woods, ropes at the ready. The owners of the farm, Tucker and Missy Jenkins, had gone into town to purchase supplies for the upcoming weekend barbecue, or they'd be saddled up and rope-ready too.

Ben whistled as he ducked under a tree branch. A rustling sound to his left drew his attention, and he had one of the New York devil-horses roped a few seconds later. One of them, though, eluded all the brothers until finally Ben couldn't take it anymore.

"How about I take these four back?" he asked Sam, trying to make it sound like he didn't care if he went or not. But he feared that if he didn't go in the next five minutes, he wouldn't even have time to scarf down a single bite of pretzel before his meeting with the recreational director.

He searched his memory for her name but came up blank. While he and his brothers had arrived at Steeple Ridge at the end of last summer, he didn't get into town for much more than church. And even then, he didn't always attend.

There was something soothing and peaceful about the woods, and sometimes the Sabbath simply found him communing with nature, which allowed him to feel closer to God. It had taken him a good five years to accept that God was still loving, still wise and omnipotent, after his parents' plane crash. Sometimes being outside with only trees, birds, and sky reminded him of God's power better than anything a pastor could say.

"Go on, then," Sam said. "Darren, you stay with me. Logan, help 'im get those horses properly secured. Lots of water."

In another situation, Ben might have asked if his brother thought any of the horses had already consumed something poisonous out in the woods, but today, he didn't. He simply set Willow toward the farm and urged her to go a little faster than he would have normally.

"Is there a fire?" Logan asked, coming up beside him.

"I made pretzels," Ben said.

Logan laughed, a big, boisterous sound that filled the sky with noise—and Ben's blood with annoyance. "You and your pretzels."

"I don't see you complaining when you eat them." Ben nudged Willow again and she almost picked up her trot.

"Nope," Logan said. "Never will. I don't know how you get them so stretchy and crispy at the same time. It's amazing."

Some of the tension drained from Ben's shoulders, and he grinned at his next oldest brother.

"Ah, spicy brown mustard," Logan said. "We have some, right?"

"Dunno." Sam did all the grocery shopping for the

brothers. "If you put it on the list at some point, I'm sure we do."

They arrived back on the farm and got the horses brushed down and properly secured in their box stalls. By the time Ben had Willow safe and secure, the very idea of a pretzel had faded to a dot on the horizon. Because he was now late for his appointment.

Sure enough, when he exited the barn, a shiny black sedan sat in the public parking lot. The car looked like it had never been on a farm.

"There you are."

He turned at the feminine voice to find a tall, athletic brunette striding away from the house and toward him. She'd definitely never been on a farm either. Ben drank in the length of her legs, very aware of the pinch of interest in his chest. Her dark brown ponytail swung from side to side, and Ben wondered what her hair would feel like between his fingers.

He swallowed. This woman was so far out of his league, he couldn't even get there in a rocket ship. She paused a healthy distance from him, cocked her hip, and folded her arms. "Which one of you is Ben?"

He glanced at Logan, who wore an expression of half-horror, half-surprise. "He is." Logan hooked his thumb at Ben and walked toward the house. Once he'd passed the beautiful woman, he turned back and beamed for all he was worth, lifting both arms in victory. "I'll save you a pretzel!" he called before turning around and hurrying into the house.

Ben waved at him like it was no big deal, that pretzels didn't matter at all That river of desire built into something bigger even as he tried to tame it. "I've forgotten your name," he said. "Missy told me, but." He laughed, the sound so full of nerves he wondered how his brothers had ever figured out how to talk to a woman, hold hands with a woman, kiss a woman. Not that they dated all that much, but Sam had had a girlfriend or two, and Logan was definitely a charmer. He could talk to women all day, and Ben had watched him do it, trying to discover the secret. So far, he hadn't figured much out.

His stomach twisted and his mouth went dry dry dry. He'd just forgotten his own name, let alone hers.

"Reagan Cantwell," she said, coming forward again. She extended her hand toward him to shake. He did, trying not to notice the softness of her skin or the strength in her touch. Or the beauty in the lines of her face. Or the depth of her eyes.

She existed on another planet, where men with a lot of money existed. More talent. More brain cells.

"My friends call me Rae."

"Like a ray of sunshine." He smiled but when she didn't, he wiped it from his face quickly, pure foolishness flooding him.

"So Missy tells me you'll have all the info on the horse-back riding lessons she wants the rec center to sponsor."

When he stood there, his thoughts stampeding like those crazy New York horses, she lifted her eyebrows as if to say *Well?*

Ben stumbled back a couple of steps. "The horseback riding lessons. Right. Yes. I know about that." And though he didn't really know what a partnership would look like, he walked forward, drew in a deep breath of her scent and got a nose full of angel food cake and chocolate.

His mouth watered but he still managed to say, "I have all the details in the office in the house. You want to come in?" He'd never been more relieved than when she came with him. And the folder Missy had put on the desk in the office really calmed him. So he hadn't looked at it yet. He could wing this meeting—as long as he didn't look directly at Rae. If he did, he might not even remember how to ride.

Reagan Cantwell couldn't believe she'd let Missy persuade her out to Steeple Ridge, even if they'd been friends for two decades. She didn't fit here; she never had. And she was needed badly at the Sports Complex, where a teen softball tournament was set to start the following day. It was Rae's job to ensure the fifty-five acre outdoor facility was ready for the swarms of people about to descend upon it. That meant no trash on any of the twenty-eight soccer fields, lots of extra paper towels and supplies for the restrooms, stocking and staffing the concession stands, and ensuring the five baseball fields were raked and ready.

She sighed as Ben opened the screen door and stood back, waiting for her to enter. The scent of baking bread and salt met her nose, reminding her that she hadn't eaten lunch yet though it was nearly time for dinner.

Rae managed the entire complex and the twenty-two-man crew it took to maintain it. She rarely sat down to eat, though she did have an office at the recreation center in town. Now that May had arrived, Rae's job was in full swing and would be until the end of August.

"Something smells good," she said, giving the cute cowboy the smile he'd sought earlier.

His grin returned, this time brighter than before. She liked it. Liked his straight teeth. Liked the gentle air surrounding him. Liked his tanned skin and wide shoulders and sexy, black cowboy hat.

Stop it, she told herself as she entered a kitchen where the other cowboy had already helped himself to one of the pretzels. *You're not dating a cowboy. Not again. You're not dating anyone for a while, remember?*

The other cowboy dunked a chunk of pretzel into dark brown mustard and took a bite. Rae's mouth watered and Ben squeezed past her. "You want one?"

"Oh, no." She half-laughed as she waved her hand. She swallowed her saliva but couldn't tear her eyes from the baked goods on the stovetop.

"Mustard or ketchup?" Ben asked as if she hadn't declined.

"Who eats ketchup on a pretzel?" she asked.

Ben frowned and muttered something under his breath as he used a pair of tongs to lift two pretzels onto a paper plate. He spooned a bit of mustard onto the plate and grabbed the whole ketchup bottle. "Office down the hall."

He nodded for her to go first, and she moved further into the house.

A bathroom sat on her right, with the office straight ahead. Another door waited to the left, but it was closed. She entered the office and took a seat in front of the desk while Ben set down the food and walked around to the other side.

"I like ketchup on pretzels," he said. He squirted way too much of the condiment onto another plate and snagged his pretzel from hers.

"Who made these?" Rae asked as she tore off a piece.

"I did."

Surprise flitted through her and her taste buds exploded with her first bite. A quiet moan emanated from her mouth and she relaxed for probably the first time that month.

"I didn't know cowboys could bake," she said once she'd eaten almost half of her pretzel.

"Some of us had to learn a lot of things early."

Something lingered there, just below the surface of his skin, just behind that pair of gorgeous eyes. Something Rae very much wanted to find out.

She wondered why she'd ever thought she should pawn this ridiculous idea of community horseback riding lessons —and Ben—onto someone else at the rec center. She hoped that maybe starting another relationship wouldn't shred her heart too badly. She prayed that Ben was older than twenty-one. He didn't look much older than a high school graduate....

Please, Lord, she thought. *Anything over twenty-one is acceptable, okay?*

Ben spoke in his deep, bass voice, which sent rumbles down her spine. She managed to listen as he showed her some mock registration forms and outlined how Missy wanted more kids out on the farm so they could get more youth into equestrian care than were currently interested.

"Who will do the lessons?" she asked.

"Missy will handle the beginners." He sighed, and she found frustration in his face. "I'll probably be assigned the others."

"You don't seem happy about that."

Ben ran his hand over his clean-shaven jaw and looked away. "I'm not particularly adept at horseback riding lessons."

"You can ride a horse, yes?" She cocked her head and played with the end of her ponytail. Classic flirting gestures, but Ben didn't seem to notice at all.

"Yeah, sure." He gathered all the papers and set them back in the folder before closing it. "I don't really like teenagers either." He cleared his throat and swiped his finger through a spot of ketchup on his plate.

"How much older—I mean, you're not a teenager, right?"

Ben's eyes, which had been flitting all over the place, zipped to hers. "What?"

Rae forced a laugh out of her chest and up her throat. "I mean, of course you're not a teenager." She leaned forward. "How old are you?"

Ben blinked. His mouth worked and he managed to say, "Uh…."

The fight left Rae's body. "Just nod if you're older than twenty-one."

He nodded once, twice, three times, almost like his neck couldn't do much more than that.

Relief washed through her veins, and she slumped back into her chair. "All right then." She reached for the folder, the weight of her schedule suddenly pressing on her shoulders. "I'll take this and go over it with my boss and let you know."

She stood and left the office, left the charming farmhouse with its delicious scent of cowboy and freshly baked pretzels. She made it to her car, feeling slightly less crazed than she had inside.

"Not dating," she muttered to herself as she slid into the car and put Steeple Ridge in her rearview mirror. With every passing yard, her erratic feelings over the cowboy settled and that sense of dread that had been plaguing her since Missy had called and set up the appointment returned. Honestly, it was better than that fiery attraction between her and a cowboy that had to be just barely older than twenty-one.

———

"Call Zackary McCoy," she instructed her car as she maneuvered back into the populated part of Island Park. The Sports Complex sat on the northern side, just across the street from the elementary school, and she set her car in that direction.

"What's up, Rae?" Zack answered, then immediately continued a conversation with someone with him wherever he was. Probably in his office, which sat right across the hall from hers.

Rae waited for him to finish, then said, "Who else can take on these horseback riding lessons?" As much as she wanted to be in Ben's presence and learn about what he hid behind those shuttered eyes, she thought their working together wouldn't be a smart idea. And now that she was thirty-five, she needed to be smart about a lot of things she hadn't considered in the past.

Zack exhaled, the sound one long hiss over the phone line. "I can check our staff, but we're already in the weeds with lifeguards, pool concessions, the senior citizen class, the—"

"All right." Rae's words had more bite than she liked, but she couldn't help it. Heading into summer was the worst time for the community rec center in terms of staffing, and Rae knew it. She'd been the human resources administrator for three years before moving over to manage the youth sports programs, and eventually, the Sports Complex.

"Let's see where we are in the next three weeks," Zack said in his placating tone. Out of all the men she'd dated in Island Park, her relationship with him had been the best. Absolutely no spark between them, which allowed them to remain friends all these years later. But she still missed the camaraderie, the feeling of belonging to someone, the assumption that she wouldn't have to eat alone that night. Or worse, with her equally single mother. Sure, she loved her mother. Liked spending Sunday afternoons with her. But Friday night? Rae didn't quite want *that* relationship with her mom.

"I'm at the Sports Complex," Rae said, though she was still several blocks away and ended the call. She really didn't have time to create, conceptualize, and carry out the horseback riding lessons. She wouldn't have time even if she somehow figured out how to clone herself. Even though she'd been a champion show rider once, she hadn't been on a horse in years and years. Had no desire to saddle up again.

No desire to give her heart to another cowboy only to have it handed back in tatters.

She pulled into the parking lot and came to a stop in the circle drive closest to the restrooms and the children's playground. She should've gone around through the neighborhood to the east, parked over by the supply shed on the edge of the complex. But she needed the walk, the fresh air, and with any luck, she'd be able to sort through her tangled emotions before she had to meet with her guys.

The sunshine warmed her skin where the air conditioning had cooled it. The spring smell of pollen lingered in the air, and the evidence that her crew had been working most of the day showed in the pristine, green lawns, free from trash and weeds. A breeze played with her ponytail and she took several deep breaths, her thoughts calming with every step she took around the mile and a quarter loop.

Her gaze wandered to a lower spot of grass that had once been a pond. The town filled it in the summer before she'd taken over the complex after a four-year-old boy had drowned in the murky water. His mother still lived in town, and Rae was glad the constant reminder didn't exist anymore. She almost made a mental note to go visit Bonnie and see how she was doing. Maybe in November….

She arrived at the supply shed, where three city trucks were parked. Her full crew should be here, as she was twenty minutes late. Sure enough, when she stepped from sun to shadow, a wall of male sweat hit her. They'd been working in the sun all day, that was certain.

Burke, her foreman, handed her a clipboard and said, "Fertilizer and pesticide applied. All trash liners filled and replaced. Bathrooms stocked. Extra help coming tomorrow. All of it."

She pretended to look at the paperwork she'd left with him that morning. A huge checklist of everything that needed to be accomplished before the two dozen softball teams arrived. "Thanks, Burke." She glanced up and looked at all the men who'd put in full days for five solid weeks to get the sports complex looking brand new after a harsh winter. "Thank you, all."

Rae smiled. "Zack and I are buying pizza for everyone tomorrow. At the rec center. Hour-long lunches for every-one." She handed the clipboard back to Burke, who hung it on a nail by the door she'd walked through. She'd ask him about the supplies that needed refreshing after the others had left. Or maybe through a text tonight.

He handed her a single sheet of paper. "What we need to restock the shed."

She took it and let her hand fall back to her side. "Burke, do you know anything about horses?"

Confusion crossed his expression. "A bit." He watched her with his hazel eyes, something sharp there that unsettled Rae.

"Enough to help me organize a riding program?"

His eyebrows rose. "Don't we have enough to do?"

She gripped the paper a bit too tight, and the crinkling sound alerted her to her stress. She relaxed her fingers, completely overwhelmed by the many tasks that needed doing.

"Monday morning," she said, tucking the paper into the back pocket of her jeans. "Come by my office for an hour." She turned her attention to the group at large, who had finished cleaning up the shed and were waiting for five o'clock to hit.

"Go on home, guys," she said a full fifteen minutes early. Her plans to stop by the diner and get dinner for her and her mother solidified when Burke and every other male in the building hung up jackets and tool belts and keys to riding lawn mowers and left.

Only minutes later, she stood in the supply shed, glancing around at the city-owned equipment, the desk where the men turned in their timecards so they could get paid, the pegs that held shovels and rakes and extra sprinkler heads.

Loneliness descended on her in the silence that

followed. She locked up and completed the loop back to her car, grateful for the blue sky and the longer evenings before darkness claimed another day.

She drove the two blocks to the rec center, which bustled with activity as townspeople came to exercise after they finished work, as the older youth volleyball program continued, as moms and little children left to head home to start dinner and get to bed.

She joined the flow of people into the building and stepped behind the desk. Down the hall, past a few doors, she finally came to her office. The youth soccer teams needed to be formed, and coaches contacted, and schedules for practices and games and tournaments made. Rae had ten days to get it all done, and she'd never completed the job faster than that.

She collected the file box containing hundreds of forms and heaved it onto her hip. If she had work to do, her mother wouldn't talk for too long about her job at the drug store, though Rae usually liked the stories. People were fascinating, and sometimes what her mother saw was stranger than fiction.

"Going home?" Meredith asked from her perch at the check-in desk.

"Going to my mother's." Rae used a dry tone that caused Meredith to chuckle. She could laugh because she had a husband and two dogs at home, waiting to fill her lonely hours with conversation and pet tricks and love.

"Have fun," Meredith singsonged. Rae had moved around the desk and was heading toward the exit when

Meredith added, "Oh, and we're still on for tomorrow, right? It's salsa night for bunko."

"Cinco de Mayo was last week." Rae half-turned and smiled at her friend. Of course she hadn't forgotten about bunko, especially if there was going to be copious amounts of salsa. They'd play loud Mexican music and eat too many chips and for one night, Rae wouldn't be so lonely it choked her.

"It's the monthly theme." Meredith brushed back her blonde hair. "Denny's going to Boston for the weekend, and Layla's bringing her famous mango salsa."

"Layla better not bring another stray dog and somehow convince me to take it home with me." She already had three cats and two dogs and she had nowhere else to put another living creature.

"I will tell her no dogs." Meredith made an X in the air in front of her.

"Or cats."

"No dogs or cats. Or ferrets. No animals, period." Meredith grinned. "Can you bring your mother's almond punch?"

Rae tipped her head back and laughed. It felt good to be reminded that she *did* have friends in Island Park. She simply didn't want to go home with her friends. "You're never getting that recipe. My mom's made me promise on my grave."

A mischievous glint sparkled in Meredith's eyes. "A girl can keep trying."

Rae lifted her hand in a final farewell and left the rec

center, finally feeling more like herself than she had since meeting with Ben Buttars that afternoon.

Read HER RESTLESS COWBOY today! Can she figure out how to put what matters most in her life—family and faith —above her job before she loses Ben?

Scan the QR code below to get it!

The Redesigned Ranch (Book 1): Jace Lovell, still nursing a wounded heart after being jilted at the altar, has dedicated himself to becoming the best foreman at Horseshoe Home Ranch. When he decides to hire an interior designer to please the ranch owner's wife, he didn't expect to be faced with a familiar face from his past. **Can Belle's patience and faith help Jace find the path to forgiveness and lead them to discover their own slice of happily-ever-after?**

Snowed in with the Cowboy (Book 2): Sterling Maughan, once a renowned snowboarder, is in self-imposed exile at his family cabin after a tragic accident stole his career. Lost and without purpose, solitude is his only companion until an unexpected visitor disrupts his isolation. **Can Norah trust Sterling enough to let him into her life and give their unexpected and forbidden love a chance?**

The Preacher's Daughter (Book 3): Landon Edmunds, a cowboy born and bred, has had his rodeo dreams realized and then dashed by a career-ending injury. Back in his hometown working at Horseshoe Home Ranch, he yearns for a new beginning with a ranch of his own. His sights are set on buying a horse ranch to train rodeo horses, but his plans take a detour when his high school best friend, Megan Palmer, steps back into his life. **Will they choose to follow their hearts, or will they let true love slip through their fingers again?**

Be sure to check out the spinoff series, the Brush Creek Cowboys romances after you read THE PREACHER'S DAUGHTER. Start with BRUSH CREEK COWBOY.

The Cowboy and the Nanny (Book 4): Twelve years ago, Owen Carr traded his roots and his sweetheart in Gold Valley for the bright lights of Nashville, where he found fame as a country music star. But when a tragic accident leaves him single-handedly raising his eight-year-old niece, Marie, he's forced to return home. Overwhelmed and out of his depth, Owen finds a lifeline in a most unexpected place. **As they mend bridges and explore the sparks that still sizzle between them, will they open their hearts to a second chance at love?**

Right Cowboy, Right Time (Book 5): Caleb Chamberlain, a fun-loving cowboy at Horseshoe Home Ranch, has spent the last five years wrestling with the ghosts of his past—a devastating breakup, alcoholism, and a near-fatal accident. Now, he's finally found solace in laughter and the rhythmic simplicity of ranch life. But a chance encounter with a familiar face threatens to upheave his newfound peace. **Can they navigate the shadows of the past to find their happily-ever-after?**

Second Chance Family (Book 6): Ty Barker has been living a carefree existence for the last thirty years. As friends around him found love and started families, Ty filled his time by giving horseback riding lessons and serving on a community service committee. But beneath the jovial surface, he's starting to feel the sting of loneliness. **He knows he wants River Lee in his life—but the question is, can he navigate the delicate steps needed to make her stay with him?**

The Christmas Cowboy Competition (Book 7): Archer Bailey has already had to yield one job to Emersyn "Emery" Enders. So when the opportunity of a cowhand job at Horseshoe Home Ranch presents itself, he keeps it to himself. Emery, whose temporary job is ending but whose responsibilities towards her physically disabled sister aren't, is left in the dark.

As the festive season unfolds, **will Emery and Archer navigate the complexities of the ranch, their close living arrangements, and their personal challenges to discover the love building between them? Or will their rivalry rob them of the greatest Christmas gift of all—true love?**

Love at First Cowboy (Book 8): Elliott Hawthorne, a career cowboy, has just witnessed his best friend and cabinmate forsake bachelorhood for matrimony. He'd be joyous if he weren't so green with envy. When a call about a family accident demands his presence, Elliott finds himself rushing from the ranch to his parents' house to see what's going on with his daddy, where he encounters the most stunning woman he's ever laid eyes on. **But as they encounter the complex dynamics of family responsibilities and personal desires, can their love-at-first-sight grow strong enough withstand the test of time?**

Her Billionaire Cowboy (Book 1): Tucker Jenkins has had enough of tall buildings, traffic, and has traded in his technology firm in New York City for Steeple Ridge Horse Farm in rural Vermont. Missy Marino has worked at the farm since she was a teen, and she's always dreamed of owning it. But her ex-husband left her with a truckload of debt, making her fantasies of owning the farm unfulfilled. Tucker didn't come to the country to find a new wife, but he supposes a woman could help him start over in Steeple Ridge. Will Tucker and Missy be able to navigate the shaky ground between them to find a new beginning?

Her Restless Cowboy: A Butters Brothers Novel, Steeple Ridge Romance (Book 2): Ben Buttars is the youngest of the four Buttars brothers who come to Steeple Ridge Farm, and he finally feels like he's landed somewhere he can make a life for himself. Reagan Cantwell is a decade older than Ben and the recreational direction for the town of Island Park. Though Ben is young, he knows what he wants—and that's Rae. Can she figure out how to put what matters most in her life—family and faith—above her job before she loses Ben?

Her Faithful Cowboy: A Butters Brothers Novel, Steeple Ridge Romance (Book 3): Sam Buttars has spent the last decade making sure he and his brothers stay together. They've been at Steeple Ridge for a while now, but with the youngest married and happy, the siren's call to return to his parents' farm in Wyoming is loud in Sam's ears. He'd just go if it weren't for beautiful Bonnie Sherman, who roped his heart the first time he saw her. Do Sam and Bonnie have the faith to find comfort in each other instead of in the people who've already passed?

Her Mistletoe Cowboy: A Butters Brothers Novel, Steeple Ridge Romance (Book 4): Logan Buttars has always been good-natured and happy-go-lucky. After watching two of his brothers settle down, he recognizes a void in his life he didn't know about. Veterinarian Layla Guyman has appreciated Logan's friendship and easy way with animals when he comes into the clinic to get the service dogs. But with his future at Steeple Ridge in the balance, she's not sure a relationship with him is worth the risk. Can she rely on her faith and employ patience to tame Logan's wild heart?

Her Patient Cowboy: A Butters Brothers Novel, Steeple Ridge Romance (Book 5): Darren Buttars is cool, collected, and quiet—and utterly devastated when his girlfriend of nine months, Farrah Irvine, breaks up with him because he wanted her to ride her horse in a parade. But Farrah doesn't ride anymore, a fact she made very clear to Darren. She returned to her childhood home with so much baggage, she doesn't know where to start with the unpacking. Darren's the only Buttars brother who isn't married, and he wants to make Island Park his permanent home—with Farrah. Can they find their way through the heartache to achieve a happily-ever-after together?

Second Chance Ranch: A Three Rivers Ranch Romance™ (Book 1): After his deployment, injured and discharged Major Squire Ackerman returns to Three Rivers Ranch, wanting to forgive Kelly for ignoring him a decade ago. He'd like to provide the stable life she needs, but with old wounds opening and a ranch on the brink of financial collapse, it will take patience and faith to make their second chance possible.

Third Time's the Charm: A Three Rivers Ranch Romance™ (Book 2): First Lieutenant Peter Marshall has a truckload of debt and no way to provide for a family, but Chelsea helps him see past all the obstacles, all the scars. With so many unknowns, can Pete and Chelsea develop the love, acceptance, and faith needed to find their happily ever after?

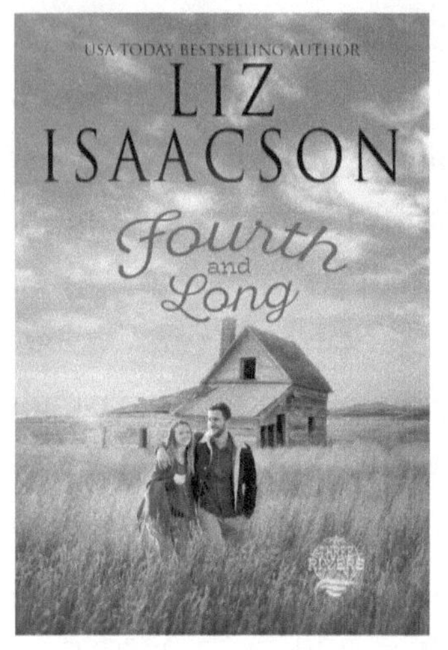

Fourth and Long: A Three Rivers Ranch Romance™ (Book 3): Commander Brett Murphy goes to Three Rivers Ranch to find some rest and relaxation with his Army buddies. Having his ex-wife show up with a seven-year-old she claims is his son is anything but the R&R he craves. Kate needs to make amends, and Brett needs to find forgiveness, but are they too late to find their happily ever after?

Fifth Generation Cowboy: A Three Rivers Ranch Romance™ (Book 4): Tom Lovell has watched his friends find their true happiness on Three Rivers Ranch, but everywhere he looks, he only sees friends. Rose Reyes has been bringing her daughter out to the ranch for equine therapy for months, but it doesn't seem to be working. Her challenges with Mari are just as frustrating as ever. Could Tom be exactly what Rose needs? Can he remove his friendship blinders and find love with someone who's been right in front of him all this time?

Sixth Street Love Affair: A Three Rivers Ranch Romance™ (Book 5): After losing his wife a few years back, Garth Ahlstrom thinks he's ready for a second chance at love. But Juliette Thompson has a secret that could destroy their budding relationship. Can they find the strength, patience, and faith to make things work?

The Seventh Sergeant: A Three Rivers Ranch Romance™ (Book 6): Life has finally started to settle down for Sergeant Reese Sanders after his devastating injury overseas. Discharged from the Army and now with a good job at Courage Reins, he's finally found happiness—until a horrific fall puts him right back where he was years ago: Injured and depressed. Carly Watters, Reese's new veteran care coordinator, dislikes small towns almost as much as she loathes cowboys. But she finds herself faced with both when she gets assigned to Reese's case. Do they have the humility and faith to make their relationship more than professional?

Eight Second Ride: A Three Rivers Ranch Romance™ (Book 7): Ethan Greene loves his work at Three Rivers Ranch, but he can't seem to find the right woman to settle down with. When sassy yet vulnerable Brynn Bowman shows up at the ranch to recruit him back to the rodeo circuit, he takes a different approach with the barrel racing champion. His patience and newfound faith pay off when a friendship--and more--starts with Brynn. But she wants out of the rodeo circuit right when Ethan wants to rejoin. Can they find the path God wants them to take and still stay together?

The Ninth Inning: A Three Rivers Ranch Romance™ (Book 8): The Christmas season has never felt like such a burden to boutique owner Andrea Larsen. But with Mama gone and the holidays upon her, Andy finds herself wishing she hadn't been so quick to judge her former boyfriend, cowboy Lawrence Collins. Well, Lawrence hasn't forgotten about Andy either, and he devises a plan to get her out to the ranch so they can reconnect. Do they have the faith and humility to patch things up and start a new relationship?

Ten Days in Town: A Three Rivers Ranch Romance™ (Book 9): Sandy Keller is tired of the dating scene in Three Rivers. Though she owns the pancake house, she's looking for a fresh start, which means an escape from the town where she grew up. When her older brother's best friend, Tad Jorgensen, comes to town for the holidays, it is a balm to his weary soul. A helicopter tour guide who experienced a near-death experience, he's looking to start over too--but in Three Rivers. Can Sandy and Tad navigate their troubles to find the path God wants them to take--and discover true love--in only ten days?

Eleven Year Reunion: A Three Rivers Ranch Romance™ (Book 10): Pastry chef extraordinaire, Grace Lewis has moved to Three Rivers to help Heidi Ackerman open a bakery in Three Rivers. Grace relishes the idea of starting over in a town where no one knows about her failed cupcakery. She doesn't expect to run into her old high school boyfriend, Jonathan Carver. A carpenter working at Three Rivers Ranch, Jon's in town against his will. But with Grace now on the scene, Jon's thinking life in Three Rivers is suddenly looking up. But with her focus on baking and his disdain for small towns, can they make their eleven year reunion stick?

The Twelfth Town: A Three Rivers Ranch Romance™ (Book 11): Newscaster Taryn Tucker has had enough of life on-screen. She's bounced from town to town before arriving in Three Rivers, completely alone and completely anonymous-- just the way she now likes it. She takes a job cleaning at Three Rivers Ranch, hoping for a chance to figure out who she is and where God wants her. When she meets happy-go-lucky cowhand Kenny Stockton, she doesn't expect sparks to fly. Kenny's always been "the best friend" for his female friends, but the pull between him and Taryn can't be denied. Will they have the courage and faith necessary to make their opposite worlds mesh?

Lucky Number Thirteen: A Three Rivers Ranch Romance™ (Book 12): Tanner Wolf, a rodeo champion ten times over, is excited to be riding in Three Rivers for the first time since he left his philandering ways and found religion. Seeing his old friends Ethan and Brynn is therapuetic--until a terrible accident lands him in the hospital. With his rodeo career over, Tanner thinks maybe he'll stay in town--and it's not just because his nurse, Summer Hamblin, is the prettiest woman he's ever met. But Summer's the queen of first dates, and as she looks for a way to make a relationship with the transient rodeo star work Summer's not sure she has the fortitude to go on a second date. Can they find love among the tragedy?

The Curse of February Fourteenth: A Three Rivers Ranch Romance™ (Book 13): Cal Hodgkins, cowboy veterinarian at Bowman's Breeds, isn't planning to meet anyone at the masked dance in small-town Three Rivers. He just wants to get his bachelor friends off his back and sit on the sidelines to drink his punch. But when he sees a woman dressed in gorgeous butterfly wings and cowgirl boots with blue stitching, he's smitten. Too bad she runs away from the dance before he can get her name, leaving only her boot behind...

Fifteen Minutes of Fame: A Three Rivers Ranch Romance™ (Book 14): Navy Richards is thirty-five years of tired—tired of dating the same men, working a demanding job, and getting her heart broken over and over again. Her aunt has always spoken highly of the matchmaker in Three Rivers, Texas, so she takes a six-month sabbatical from her high-stress job as a pediatric nurse, hops on a bus, and meets with the matchmaker. Then she meets Gavin Redd. He's handsome, he's hardworking, and he's a cowboy. But is he an Aquarius too? Navy's not making a move until she knows for sure…

Sixteen Steps to Fall in Love: A Three Rivers Ranch Romance™ (Book 15): A chance encounter at a dog park sheds new light on the tall, talented Boone that Nicole can't ignore. As they get to know each other better and start to dig into each other's past, Nicole is the one who wants to run. This time from her growing admiration and attachment to Boone. From her aging parents. From herself.

But Boone feels the attraction between them too, and he decides he's tired of running and ready to make Three Rivers his permanent home. **Can Boone and Nicole use their faith to overcome their differences and find a happily-ever-after together?**

The Sleigh on Seventeenth Street: A Three Rivers Ranch Romance™ (Book 16): A cowboy with skills as an electrician tries a relationship with a down-on-her luck plumber. Can Dylan and Camila make water and electricity play nicely together this Christmas season? Or will they get shocked as they try to make their relationship work?

The First Lady of Three Rivers Ranch: A Three Rivers Ranch Romance™ (Book 17): Heidi Duffin has been dreaming about opening her own bakery since she was thirteen years old. She scrimped and saved for years to afford baking and pastry school in San Francisco. And now she only has one year left before she's a certified pastry chef.

Frank Ackerman's father has recently retired, and he's taken over the largest cattle ranch in the Texas Panhandle. A horseman through and through, he's also nearing thirty-one and looking for someone to bring love and joy to a homestead that's been dominated by men for a decade. But when he convinces Heidi to come clean the cowboy cabins, she changes all that. But the siren's call of a bakery is still loud in Heidi's ears, even if she's also seeing a future with Frank. Can she rely on her faith in ways she's never had to before or will their relationship end when summer does?

Eighteen Bowties and Counting: A Three Rivers Ranch Romance™ (Book 18): He's her older brother's best friend and completely off-limits. She's got a way with horses...and a heart condition. Can Beau and Charlotte navigate close quarters to find their happily-ever-after?

ABOUT LIZ

Liz Isaacson writes inspirational romance, usually set in Texas, or Wyoming, or anywhere else horses and cowboys exist. She lives in Utah, where she writes full-time, takes her two dogs to the park everyday, and eats a lot of veggies while writing. Find her on her website at feelgoodfiction-books.com

www.ingramcontent.com/pod-product-compliance
Lightning Source LLC
Chambersburg PA
CBHW050332110726
47899CB00007B/2465